GRANDMA VS. THE TORNADO

AND OTHER STORIES FROM THE LAST STOP RETIREMENT COMMUNITY

OTHER BOOKS BY KIRT J BOYD

THE LAST STOP

FOR KRISTEN,

WHO MAKES ME LAUGH EVERY DAY.

Grandma vs. the Tornado

And Other Stories from The Last Stop Retirement Community

KIRT J BOYD

ROLLING DOWN THE MOUNTAIN PRESS

INTRODUCTORY REMARKS

It's that time again! Time to look back and reflect on all the wonderful, strange, hilarious, and tragic (sometimes) things that took place at our little retirement home on the hill . . . There is no hill. That's why it's funny. If you don't believe us, describe it that way to new visitors and watch the confused look that comes over their faces when they start looking around for some sort of view. By the same token, if you leave out the river, the paths, the horse barn, and the one-lane bridge, they'll be further confused because you failed to mention them. This is for the best. We feel it's much better to let them discover those things for themselves. We've yet to meet a person who doesn't have a soft spot for a one-lane bridge, and if we ever come across one, we'll let you know so you can hide your valuables.

What follows is a much longer version of the Year in Review that normally appears with your Last Stop Bulletin, the first week of the new year. We've had so much fun writing it in the past that we've decided to do a much longer, extended version this year. Keep in mind that this is our first attempt, so we're still feeling things out. If it's a bit clumsy in places, well, you'll just have to learn to live with it.

The stories herein are taken from personal experience, eye witness accounts, and interviews with those directly involved. Where details seem a bit far-fetched, we have done our best to verify the facts, though we didn't try all that hard because then the stories might turn out to be a lot less entertaining.

Also, please keep in mind that memories, ours included, are a bit shoddy these days, so if we have you wearing a red dress when you were actually wearing blue shorts, we're sorry, but if that's going to get you all bent out of shape, you might want to pass this on to someone with a sense of humor.

Rest assured that we have done our best. The spirit is there, and that's what counts.

On a similar note, where those involved are doing things that are shady, silly, or downright dumb, we've tried to be gentle, but our "gentle" can be a bit prickly, or so we've been told. If you find yourself offended by something we've written, remember that we love you; we just don't know quite how to show it.

And finally, an apology to all of those we've left out. The truth is that many, many interesting, funny, enlightening, or otherwise notable things happen at our little community every day, and there will no doubt be a few of you who will feel there was some incident that you were involved in that was worth mentioning and will be hurt that it was left out. We've left it out simply because our love of trees prevents us from putting everything down on paper. If it makes you feel better, we will not be including all the weekly bulletins from the previous year, either, but have chosen the four that best sum up each season. Besides, it would be redundant and self indulgent, and, if we're honest, not all of them contain our best work. Coming up with fifty two interesting, funny, or otherwise helpful weather reports, for instance, is not as easy as it looks, and though it pains us to admit it, there have been times when we've sort of dialed it in. But enough moaning. Much like the bulletin, we are the authors of this rag, so it is what it is, and if you want to complain about it, throw it in the suggestion box.

So, welcome family and friends and local rubbish collectors. Let's get started!

--The Chin-wags

FALL

The Last Stop Bulletin

The Weather Front

Well, fall is here and there's nothing we can do about it. And if that isn't dreary enough for you, just glance out your window any day this week and you'll be treated to gloom enough for two. Those wishing to see the bright side of things might be tempted to speculate that all the rain we've been having lately will go a long way in filling up our reservoirs. But Greg and Kathy on the 9 o'clock news would like to remind you that despite the pools of standing water leaving drivers stranded all over the state, we're still in a drought, and unless we get a hundred and eight feet of snow in the next five months we'll soon be recycling our own water. You like that? Summer just ended and they're already talking about next summer's watering restrictions.

Which leads us to our tip of the day: Stop watching the news; you'll probably live longer.

You Ought to Know

The first thing you ought to know is that we tend to get cranky the first week of fall. If you need evidence, go back and reread the weather front. While we stand behind its accuracy, we must admit it's a bit bitter. The fact that we just wrote, "a bit bitter," has now made us angry. We blame fall.

On a completely unrelated note, the new outlet mall opened last week, so we'll be adding a stop to the Tuesday shopping trips. Because of this, we suggest you get to the lobby early. Randy has been given strict instructions to leave at exactly 8 a.m., so no stragglers.

ACCORDING TO ROGER

We are not Roger. Let's just get that out of the way first. Since this is the first appearance of this column, we thought some introductory notes were in order. The Roger in the title is our very own Roger Willow. Roger has been harassing us about the need for the MALE perspective for the last several years, so . . . after much consideration, we have decided to grudgingly open the door to a new voice, though we've warned him that if he says something silly we won't hold back in our criticism.

He was supposed to have copy for us this morning, but we haven't seen anything yet. Don't worry, if he starts missing deadlines we'll start reviewing feminine hygiene products in his name.

NOTES FROM THE MAINTENANCE SHED

For the umpteenth time, the picnic area is not a dumping ground. If you bring something to the picnic area, the wildlife, the ozone, and the sanctity of our rivers would appreciate it if you would take the leftover food and containers out with you. Also, Harry considers bits of bread and nuts just as offensive as trash, so if you plan on feeding the wildlife, make sure there are enough of them around to finish the meal. Harry has a tendency to overreact when it comes to trash, so what set him off may have been a gum wrapper that blew in from the subdivision on the other side of the river. If this is the case, we apologize, but it's better to be safe.

You may have noticed by the undeniable Chin-wag tone that Harry is no longer writing this column himself. We are now taking his notes and complaints and composing them into our own finely crafted words. Harry is a man of few words, and he's a man of even fewer words in print. There's only so many times we can publish, "Trash!" before it starts getting redundant.

KELLY'S CORNER

We should have seen this coming, but Kelly is no longer the author of Kelly's Corner. Ahem. Maybe there's something in the water. But unlike Harry, Kelly is a woman of many, many words, most of them containing four letters. And since she has found it difficult to omit the colorful language, we have decided to do it for her. Now she just swings by our office, yells at us for a few minutes, and then goes away. She has been ominously silent since the change. This might be a good week to take your exercising outdoors.

THE HOT SEAT

All right, Mr. Langley. We tried to warn you. We know that propping open the lobby door to bring your groceries in is convenient, but it's October now, so when you open the door, all the dead leaves come in with the groceries. About seven trees worth blew in here yesterday, and if you could have seen the look on Harry's face, it would have stood your hair on end. He said something about drowning the next person who leaves the door open. Harry chooses his words carefully, that's all we're saying.

GUEST COLUMN

In the spirit of trying new things, we are starting a guest column, cleverly titled "Guest Column." The format is open for the time being. We're not interested in doing any more editing than we already do, so brush up on your grammar and syntax before submitting. We refuse to publish anything inappropriate, illiterate, or written in crayon. Laugh if you must, but suggestion box entries occasionally show up this way, so we know you're out there. We realize that the occasional misspelled word or wayward comma is bound to creep in, but if you spell stop with two p's, we will purposely leave it in and highlight it in big bold letters.

THE SUGGESTION BOX

You have spoken and we have listened . . . sort of. We admit that we picked through the suggestion box notes rather quickly this morning because of all the other columns going on, but there seems to be quite a few of you suggesting we tone down the sarcasm. So much so that it feels like a coordinated effort. Now that we look at them again, the handwriting looks remarkably similar. We don't know who you are, but if you're going to try this sort of vote-tampering thing, we suggest you do more to hide your identity than by using different colored ink. Maybe you should try wording the suggestions differently, or at least try to disguise the fact that all your S's have an unnecessary little squiggly line, suggesting you got distracted from what you were doing and started doodling.

HOLY MOSES!

Halloween is right around the corner, so we need to start thinking about a costume for Holy Moses. We all remember how much he disliked being a pumpkin last year, so let's try to come up with something that has a little more teeth to it.

GRANDMA VS. THE TORNADO

It started with a tornado warning. It was October 5th. We know this because it was the day of the annual soccer game, which was being temporarily postponed because of torrential rain. October? Tornadoes? Old people playing soccer? Some of you not familiar with our little community might be confused, so we'll take a moment to clear things up.

First, the soccer game is played in October for one very simple reason: the first annual soccer game was played in October, and what's the point of having a tradition if the date is always changing? And it's not so strange when you think about it. While we love summer, we're not fond of extreme heat, unless it involves hats, sunglasses, and umbrella drinks. In early October, the snow usually has yet to start piling up (though not always) and the memories of summer are hanging on for dear life, so it seems as good a time as any.

The next thing that might be bothering you is the idea of old people playing soccer. Yes, soccer is hard on your knees, but getting old is hard on everything. First of all, we are not old and we resent the implication. We are oldish. There's a difference. We aren't interested in spending our golden years in recliners, doing crossword puzzles and watching soaps, any more than we are interested in, say, naked mud wrestling. We are active because it makes us feel good. The minute you start acting old, you get old, and then you die, which isn't something we're interested in either.

There were sixteen players milling around the courtyard just in case the rain stopped and the game could begin. Most of them had played in years past, so they were used to playing in occasional inclement weather. A little rain, a little snow, a little hail, no problem, but when one of them noticed three families of ducks gliding through their field, even the hardiest of them started looking around for something else to do. What they came up with was an individual contest of seeing which of them could withstand the driving rain the longest.

Holy Moses, that revered and often feared canine, enjoyed the spectacle from behind one of the lobby windows. He, too, loved soccer, mostly because he could fit the ball in its entirety in his mouth. He also seemed to enjoy the stink everyone made about the ball being covered in Holy slobber, which differs from regular slobber in both quantity and consistency. But, unlike his fellow players, Holy Moses didn't get wet if he could help it, except on those rare occasions when he went down to the river to chase water skippers.

He had, in fact, been weighing his need to go to the bathroom with the likelihood that the bath team would take advantage of him already being wet and attack him with shampoo and scrub brushes, which actually wasn't an unreasonable fear. Because of Holy's size—which, at this writing, is hovering around 170lbs—the task of bathing him is much more than one person can handle, so a team was created. Other teams followed: the "Nail clipping" team, the "Take-Holy-to-the-vet" team, the "Get-Holy-outside-when-it's-snowing" team, the "Get-Holy-off-the-bed-after-he-sneaks-into-a-resident's-room" team. All the teams meet once a month to discuss strategies and tactics.

Of course, we don't actually know what Holy was thinking. It's probably more likely that he just needed to pee and was trying to decide if he should wait it out. Holy Moses is not your average canine, though, so the bath scenario is well within his capabilities.

The tornado siren, when it started blaring, oddly enough, was just a minor curiosity. Perhaps it was because of the rumor going around that the weather alert people were drunk most of the time. More than likely, though, it was because tornadoes just aren't taken that seriously around here. However terrifying the prospect of a tornado is in other parts of the country, in southwestern

Colorado, except on very rare occasions, the "tornadoes" don't usually do much more than poke out of the clouds for a quick look around before returning from which they came. The ones that do make it to the ground usually limp around, upset loose wood piles, tip over trashcans, and then pack it up and go away, which is why most of us didn't do much more that glance up at the sky and give a disappointed snort before returning to whatever it was we were doing.

No one scoffed harder or louder than Frankie Billings in room 47 of the Buena Vista wing, and for good reason. Frankie spent the first seven years of his life in a series of little farm houses outside of Wichita, Kansas. He liked to say that running from tornadoes was a sport in Kansas, and after hearing him recount close-calls, you'd swear he spent his childhood doing little else. Tornadoes were so frequent, he said, that the Visitor's Center printed maps that showed where the various tornado shelters were located around town with a little caption at the bottom that read, "When in doubt, dive in a ditch!" What you were supposed to do if there wasn't a ditch handy is anybody's guess, but we suppose running in the opposite direction might be as good a place to start as any.

Growing up, Frankie wasn't allowed to play outside unattended on days when severe weather was in the forecast. Tornadoes showed up so frequently that Frankie's parents didn't want to have to go looking for him, and, "It ain't like a tornado drives up in a van," his uncle liked to point out.

Frankie's tornado stories always ended the same way: the family, the neighbors, the dog, all loaded down with their most prized possessions, making a mad dash for the shelter. The fact that it was several hundred yards behind the house made timing crucial. It was their belief that the tornadoes were targeting them specifically, so they figured the farther away the shelter was from the main house the better. The shelter was actually just an old camper shell that Frankie's father and uncles had buried in the ground. They cut a trap door in the top of it so everyone could dive in and pull it closed behind them. This shelter traveled around with them all throughout Kansas and Oklahoma. Every time the house got destroyed, they'd dig it up and haul it with them to the next place.

Because of the vast distance between the house and the shelter, the runners had to pace themselves. If they sprinted, they were likely to tire before reaching safety. And if they opted to jog at a slow pace, well, they might find themselves having to suddenly run faster than they were capable of. Either way you were a goner. The closest any one of them had come to either scenario was the time Frankie's grandmother (a stout woman who refused to take off her heeled shoes for any reason, tornadoes included) was sucked up just as she was performing a canon ball into the shelter opening. It was only through the Harvey twins' quick and completely in unison decision to each grab one of grandma's legs that she was saved. By the time it was over, her little hat was gone and her dress was clear up over her head, but she was safe and promised to make the Harvey twins a ham and pickle sandwich just as soon as they rebuilt the house.

As much as we like this story, we sometimes wonder about its authenticity. We want to believe it. Something about grandma vs. the tornado has drama you can't find on afternoon television. We can't help wondering, though, how many little farm houses Frankie lived in growing up, and why, for crying out loud, didn't they move to a state where the tornadoes were less likely to follow them?

The tornado siren wasn't a hoax. There was indeed a funnel cloud, but it was so lethargic and timid-looking that it didn't cause much concern, though some of our soccer players had apparently watched too many reruns of *Storm Chasers*, because half of them fell all over each other trying to get inside. Maybe they were just so shocked to see an actual tornado that they panicked.

Because of Frankie's history with tornadoes, the siren was a never ending source of entertainment. It didn't matter the time of day or night, shortly after the siren started up, you'd hear faint, hysterical laughter. And if you were in close enough proximity, you'd hear some variation of the following: "This is nothing! Kansas has dust devils bigger than you!" And, as if to prove his point, he'd make his way out the nearest exit and dance on the lawn.

All of the above is what transpired within a minute of the siren sounding, with one crucial difference: Frankie wasn't wearing any clothes. He had become so excited by the threat of a tornado that

11

he went directly from the shower to the lobby to the lawn, leaving residents and visitors alike aghast.

The good thing about it was that it temporarily distracted the remaining soccer players from the fact that they could no longer feel their extremities. For some reason, Frankie was even more worked up than usual, and stood, oblivious to his nakedness, shaking his fist at the sky and daring Mother Nature to come take him. As far as we know, Frankie is the only person in the whole history of mankind that has tried to provoke a tornado.

This isn't quite as strange as it seems. Frankie's dream was to be caught up in an EF5 out in the middle of a field somewhere so he could ride it for a while. A few of us over the years tried to gently point out to him that it wasn't the wind but what was whipping around in the wind that killed you, but he laughed in a mildly disturbing way and the issue was dropped.

At various times we tried to be helpful in a sarcastic way by suggesting he take up a second career as a storm chaser. One year for Christmas we got him brochures.

"She'll find me when she's ready," he said, which was about the most cryptic thing we had ever heard.

In the end, the day of the annual soccer game would not be a day of soccer. Nor would it be the day that Frankie was carried off by his famed twister because one had finally lived up to its reputation.

As some of you know, we lost Frankie earlier this year to a very non tornado-like cardiac event. He was buried in Fairmont Cemetery. If you want to visit him, look for the headstone with the little tornadoes etched in the granite. There's no place like home.

THE LAST STOP BULLETIN

THE WEATHER FRONT

Well, everything is officially dead. We've tried to be more positive this week, but no good has come of it. Once the flip flops have gone back in the trunk, there is a sadness that seems to hang over us. There was one patch of green hanging on for dear life out by the fitness center, but now even that has given into fall's death grip. We know there are some of you weirdos that like this sort of thing, and talk endlessly about the beauty of life-cycles, but do us a favor and keep it to yourselves. The fact remains that two months ago everything was pretty and green and lush, and now everything is ugly and brown and wilted, and not even the changing of the Aspen trees is going to change our feelings on the subject. Perhaps we are victims of seasonal depression, perhaps not. Maybe it has nothing to do with everything dying and everything to do with the approaching holiday season. Who knows? Anyway, the weather is going to be pleasant enough, just try not to look around too much.

You Ought to Know

Those of you who thought you saw a blast from the past, thought right. Midnight, the untouchable kitty, has returned to us in all her hissing, snorting splendor. Midnight's keeper, Helen Watson, moved to Portland, Maine after we unceremoniously ousted her a couple of years ago, so it's impressive that Midnight presumably walked the 2,000-or-so miles cross country to get back to us. We don't know if this says more about us or more about Helen, but we're all for rewarding effort, so she's here to stay. This doesn't mean she's friendly, at least not yet, so don't try picking her up or anything silly like that. We have a feeling that Holy Moses will play a big part in her recovery, so let's all just stay back and see what happens.

According to Roger

A man is a man, they say, unless that man is a woman. (And what man wouldn't want to be a woman if given the choice?) I thought I'd start with something catchy and humorous to set the tone. Most of you know me, but for those who don't, I'm Roger (well, duh!) and I'm hoping to give a little balance to the newsletter, which seems to me to lean a little too far to the female side of things. This isn't supposed to be a debate column, so I won't be addressing anything specifically, but I will try to cover topics that appeal to men, which, in case you were wondering, is actually the dominant gender by 23 residents.

So make way for sports! (boring) and fishing! (cruel and unnecessary unless starving to death) and movies that tend to get ignored or sneered at because of the blood and guts. Our time has come!

So long for now from our little retirement home on the hill. If you have any ideas for future columns, please let me know. (First of all, we came up with the hill thing, so please don't steal our jokes. Second, do you think men actually read this? And third, you sound like a radio broadcaster.)

Notes from the Maintenance Shed

Mark today on your calendar with a big smiley face. It seems that after ranting and raving about it for the last few weeks, we have all lived up to Harry's standards when it comes to keeping the activities room free of snack remnants. We wish we could say as much for the lobby. For some reason, everyone seems to think the lobby is a cafeteria, which would imply that Harry is the lunch lady, so you understand his hostility.

Lest anyone has forgotten, the trash cans are those stainless steel numbers with the lids that say TRASH on them.

Kelly's Corner

"The stability balls aren't bouncy chairs! Some of you have gotten in the habit of using the gym as a social meeting place. This will not continue. We can always go back to doing classes only."

The actual note was several more paragraphs, but after getting rid of the expletives, this is what we were left with.

The Hot Seat

This week's hot seat recipient is whoever wrote the guest column appearing below. We have a suggestion box for a reason. Just so you know, Anonymous, Chef Amato hasn't been himself since he and his wife separated last month. This would explain why the chicken fried steak has been a little dry, so cut him some slack.

We're going to give you the benefit of the doubt and assume that you were aiming for the suggestion box and accidentally dropped it in the guest column box. The real reason you're in the hot seat is because of your anonymity. Criticizing someone from behind "—Anonymous" is just obnoxious enough to be worthy of inclusion.

The fact that we included the offensive guest column in the "Guest Column" is evidence that we're a bit short on guest column material. So don't be shy. Let it rip.

GUEST COLUMN

Am I the only one that thinks the restaurant food has taken a turn for the worse? I mean, don't get me wrong, it's usually just great, but lately the chicken fried steak has been a little dry.

—Anonymous

THE SUGGESTION BOX

You have spoken and we have listened, but we don't think that a midnight showing of *Halloween* would be a good idea. Not so much because of the movie, but because of the time slot. We feel all the extra work would ultimately be wasted because most of you would end up sleeping through it. What's so scary about a guy wearing a mask killing people with a butcher knife? We take that back. It's terrifying.

HOLY MOSES!

Well, apparently Holy Moses has a new enemy. We know how much he loves to pounce on and maul enthusiastically those who wrong him, we just didn't think he'd extend this to beetles. Some of you have noticed the rather large, and obviously angry, beetle that's been hanging out by the porch swing, and most of you have been smart enough to ogle at it and then leave it be. Some suggested killing it, which we find slightly excessive. Just because it's ugly and hisses and has big ole pincers, doesn't mean it should die. Holy apparently thinks it should be harassed into leaving. Holy only barks on special occasions, and only howls on very, very special occasions, but he's been treating us to both since the beetle showed up. Over the last few days, Holy has herded him off the porch swing and halfway out to the lawn. Maybe by this time next week he will be far enough away that Holy can go back to being the big lug over there that doesn't move much.

Die with Your Cleats on

We can't talk about the annual soccer game without mentioning everyone's favorite grouch, Luther M., whose antics that day were overshadowed by Frankie's burlesque show, but were just as noteworthy. This late in the game, you'd think we'd know his last name, but we've been calling him Luther M. for so long that the name escapes us. We'd look it up, but we're sure everyone knows the Luther M. of which we speak, since he's best known for biting people.

Luther is by far our oldest living soccer player. His first game was in 1982, where he scored three goals, one of which by way of a header that laid him out flat and required emergency resuscitation. His most notable game was the one played during the blizzard of 1984. Luther competed in every game up until 1999 when his hip began giving him fits. He continued on as head referee until he was moved up to Special Care in 2005, where he was left to watch the game from afar. We all knew how much he missed it, so we chipped in and bought him a soccer uniform so he could at least play the part. Some felt that a man his age tromping around in soccer cleats was dangerous, but we didn't have the heart to take them away from him. And even if we did think his shoes were hazardous to his health, no one wanted to be the one to have to tell him. He had been a handful even before he started biting people. The biting, by the way, never causes any significant injuries because Luther's teeth are long gone and he refuses to wear dentures, but those who've had the experience of Luther suddenly latching onto their arm and gnashing enthusiastically won't soon forget it. We tolerate his behavior and let him keep his shoes mostly because there's just something inspiring about a man with bony little legs (sorry, Luther, but we call it like we see it) pushing around a walker wearing soccer cleats.

For Christmas a few years ago, we took it up a notch and bought him a pair of high-powered binoculars. Of course, to Luther, this was a cheap replacement for the soccer ball we had to take away from him the year before. We had all underestimated Luther's ability to actually kick the ball. Virtually all staff assigned to Special Care found themselves diving for cover more often than they'd like to admit. It isn't every day that you get beamed in the head with a soccer ball while you're trying to do paperwork. So, late one night, we had Nick, one of the bigger male nurses, slip into Luther's room and wrestle it away from him while he slept. That's mostly when the biting began.

Luther has learned to appreciate the binoculars. Perhaps he's mellowing with age. Now, if you observe him watching the game through his binoculars, you'll notice his feet performing complex, imaginary ball dribbles, as if he were out there on the field. This year, we're thinking about putting together a CD of crowd noises from various sporting events so we can play it for him on game day.

Since we're on the subject of humoring Luther, we can't help but talk a little bit about our beloved, if a bit gruff, maintenance man, Harry. While Harry tends to dislike most people in general, he has a soft spot for Luther. Harry would like you to believe that he has a heart of stone, but his soft side pops up every now and then, never more so than on those days when he pedals Luther around the grounds on a mountain bike with a special trailer hitched to the back.

This all started because of Harry's habit of towing around Holy Moses. Luther saw this and thought it would be fun. We have a feeling that most of you share Luther's opinion, but are shy about asking.

If you've never seen it, there is nothing quite like the sight of a disgruntled maintenance man towing around a fully grown, hundred, and now seventy-one pound, Mastiff on a bicycle. Holy's weight has soared in recent months due to the pool of new residents who give him treats in hopes of getting on his good side. Holy only has one side, just so we're clear, but it manages to be both lovable and condescending at the same time.

This little circus act is now being included in the promotional materials as part of the entertainment. Those of you who've yet to witness this spectacle don't know what you're missing. On sunny days, after the grounds have been mowed and trimmed and watered, and the trash has been collected, Harry will often break out the bicycle. If you can, try to get a good seat. Holy has an overwhelming need to see everything at once, so his constantly shifting weight inevitably sends them zigzagging into the bushes. Harry has it somewhat easier with Luther, who tips the scale around eighty-eight pounds, and is content to keep his weight more or less centered.

There would not be a performance the day of the annual soccer game, though, because of the rain, but Luther did provide the Special Care staff their share of entertainment. While the soccer players stood huddled together waiting for the rain to stop, Luther watched them through his binoculars. One of the players noticed him up there and offered a little wave, but it wasn't returned. If the player would have heard Luther mumbling, "Rain! Hmph! This is nothing. Snow and ice, now that would be something. Cry babies!" he might not have extended the courtesy.

It wasn't long before Luther had worked himself up into a small frenzy. The nurses offered him snacks to try and calm him down, but it didn't work. Soon he was up and banging on the window, "Try kicking the ball in three feet of snow! Try finding the ball in three feet of snow!" Luther had a point. Compared to what Luther had faced, the rain was a minor inconvenience. No one was going to get frostbite. The goalie wasn't going to lose his ring finger and half his thumb like the goalie in 1984. Luther himself hadn't been able to feel his left foot for over a week after the game, and his big toe still has a bluish hue to it some thirty years later. To Luther, this wasn't even as bad as the 1993 game where they played with quarter-sized hail raining down on them. That year the nurses had to work double shifts to keep all the welts on ice.

Luther settled down when the tornado siren started going off, but when he looked up at the sky and saw the little, wobbling nub that had inspired the siren, he was once again on his feet and banging on the window. And when he saw half of the players shelter their heads and run inside, Luther dropped the binoculars, stood up abruptly, swiveled his walker towards the door and informed everyone who would listen, "I'll show them a thing or two about playing in inclement—" but he stopped short, having caught Frankie out the corner of his eye in all his naked glory, yelling at the heavens. Luther smiled for the first time that morning. "Now there is a man of character!"

THE LAST STOP BULLETIN

THE WEATHER FRONT

It's heeeeeere! We knew it wouldn't last forever, and just in time for Halloween. We don't know how many times the first snow has fallen on Halloween, but it seems like a bunch, and this year is no different. It's not going to be a blizzard or anything, but we should see several inches out of it, so if you talk to your grandkids, make sure they bundle up. Flurries will start late Wednesday night and will pick up Thursday morning, so any of you planning on dressing up as ballerinas or cheerleaders for Halloween might want to change your costume choice to one that has a few more layers to it. The first part of the week, on the other hand, is going to be gorgeous. Yes, we admit it, the fall colors can be pretty in small doses.

YOU OUGHT TO KNOW

Many of you claim to have seen the hatchet lady of Morrison, and because we are in a Halloween kind of mood and haven't had the pleasure, we're going to pile in the transport bus this Tuesday evening and go have a look see. The story goes that if you drive down Morrison's main street and look in the rear view mirror, you will see an old lady chasing after your car with a hatchet. What she does when traffic is at a standstill is anyone's guess. It might be tricky to see her with so many of us piled in the transport bus, but we think it's worth a shot.

Also, we'll be having a Halloween costume contest in the activities room at 4 p.m. Halloween day, so if you want a shot at a $75 King Soopers gift card, shuffle on down and let's see what you've got.

ACCORDING TO ROGER

Hello friends! Ah, the changing of the seasons. A rebirth. A renewing! (Yes, he's one of them.) I know fall has been with us for a while, but I just couldn't help taking a moment to appreciate the changing of the season. Just when the heat becomes too much, it's Mother Nature to the rescue. She's funny that way.

Football season is in full swing, and our Denver Broncos are off to a rip roaring start, which might explain why I'm so giddy. Just for the record, the Broncos are going all the way this year! Go Broncos! (We must grudgingly agree with Roger. We do love our Broncos, but only the Broncos. We'd rather have our eyelids collectively stretched and snapped shut before watching the Oakland Rams, or whatever that silly horned team is called.)

In the spirit of Halloween (clever) I've decided to do a poll in today's column. The question is: Who is the scariest movie villain of all time? Just to get things rolling, I nominate Freddy Kruger, because it's not like you can knock the knives out of his hands when the knives are his hands. (Good lord.)

NOTES FROM THE MAINTENANCE SHED

It's that time of year again . . . We thought we'd give you a minute to figure out what we're talking about. It's the time of year when there is an excess of candy in the facility and an excess of little kids who aren't nearly as consistent as we'd like them to be when it comes to candy wrappers finding their way into the trash cans. In years past, there's also been an abundance of bubblegum found in various states of "chewed" stuck to surfaces that were never intended for bubblegum, so let's try to keep an eye on the little monsters. Yes, we know we've been harping about trash a lot lately, but we take pride in keeping our little abode shipshape.

KELLY'S CORNER

"No costumes in the gym!" That was all Kelly had for us, so we'll do our best to work out the possible reasons why. First, we guess that if you show up for your workout dressed as a big ole pumpkin, you're probably not going to take your workout very seriously and would therefore be wasting her time. Second, it's probably a safety hazard. What would happen if your big ole elf shoes got all hung up in the treadmill? Or what if your big ole witch nose accidentally poked someone in the eye when you were trying to spot them? Well, that would be a big ole problem, wouldn't it?

THE HOT SEAT

Mr. Rogers, we know your apology is sincere, but because of the emotional toll your actions took on those involved, we have no choice but to put you in the hot seat. The fact that your name is Mr. Rogers makes what you did that much worse. Instead of wearing a nonthreatening sweater like the Mr. Rogers on the television show to greet the children visiting from Porter Elementary, you chose to wear bloodstained overalls and a Michael Myers mask. The idea was to bridge the gap between the young and old through common interests, but all they found was a crazy guy in a mask waving a knife at them. We realize Halloween is coming up, but they were third graders. Maybe if they had been familiar with the *Halloween* movies they would have made the connection and wouldn't have run screaming through the halls. We'll never know. What we do know is that the media has gotten a hold of this and will likely lead with it. So now, instead of being active, charming, funny seniors that enjoy having fun just as much as the youngsters, we're officially a bunch of crazy old people who like to scare little children. Thanks, freaking Mr. Rogers.

GUEST COLUMN

This is a story I like to call The Giggling Green Goblin, and it goes like this. One day when I was at work, one hundred years ago (ha-ha) I completely forgot that it was Halloween. I thought it was strange that some of my co-workers were wearing odd hats, and others seemed to have aged horribly since I had last seen them. It didn't dawn on me until I was on my way home and started seeing all the kids walking around in costumes and carrying candy sacks. About a second after I realized it was Halloween, I realized that I had forgotten to buy candy for the kids. My street was always really popular with trick or treaters, so when I turned down my block, I wasn't surprised to see twenty- or- so kids making their way towards my house. In order to not be caught empty handed, I parked my car on the street in front of my house until they went by, cringing a little when they paused in front of the house before continuing on. I could tell they were disappointed. Once they were several houses down, I sighed with relief and then started making my way to the front door, smiling at how clever I was. I hadn't gone more than a few steps when I realized that I had overlooked one particular trick or treater: The Giggling Green Goblin.

Why he was out by himself, I have no idea, but the important thing is that he saw me walking to my door, so he knew I was home. He broke into an awkward jog. When I saw what was happening, I panicked. I thought about knocking on the door myself, acting like a visitor, but I already had my key out, poised and ready. And now he was giggling. I broke into a run, fumbling with the keys. "Tirk or Twit!" That's how it sounded because he was running and giggling at the same time. I thrust the key in and turned it the wrong way. "Tirk or Tweet!" He was closer now, and he sounded like he was getting angry. He was still giggling, but it had an edge to it. He must have sensed that I was trying to get away from him, because he broke into a run. I could hear his little footfalls pounding. The door opened and I threw myself inside just as The Giggling Green Goblin reached the door, "Tirk or Twitter!" And there, on the little table next to the door, was a bowl-full of candy, from which I grabbed handfuls and began chucking them at The Giggling Green Goblin until he was satisfied and went away.

I have my wife to thank, of course, because, while I always seemed to forget candy for the youngsters, she never did.

--Ed Bailey

THE SUGGESTION BOX

You have spoken and we have listened, but we can't justify putting up those gigantic blowup witches and ghosts on the front lawn to entertain the handful of grand children and great grandchildren that will break their Halloween routes to trick or treat here. Besides, they really aren't that scary.

HOLY MOSES!

With Halloween rapidly approaching, this is a good time to remind everyone that Holy Moses is chunky. Fat seems rude and not entirely accurate. Even he would admit that he has some junk in the trunk, but he might fight us if we went beyond that. Besides, chunky implies lovable, which isn't entirely accurate either, unless you're one of the select few. Whatever the label, the last thing in the world Holy Moses needs right now is more candy, and since there's going to be an abundance of candy around here this week, we thought we should bring it up. We will make an exception for cherry twizzlers, because we know how much he loves them, but please, for the love of everything Holy, don't feed him anything else. He already has to do three hours of cardiovascular activity just to burn the calories he's already consuming, so let's not add to it.

GET A NURSE!

As a general rule, we aren't partial to those poor souls between the ages of eighteen and thirty. It isn't that we don't like them, we just don't want to spend a lot of time with them. Kids are fine, because they're usually funny, and if they start acting up, they can be picked up and hauled off to a place where their voices are less likely to carry. Those in their thirties, forties, and fifties are generally too busy to be much of a problem, and the over sixty crowd, well, they're like family. But there's something about the teens and twenty-somethings that don't jive with some of us older folks. There seems to be a lack of understanding on both sides. We're aware that we're making an entirely unfair blanket statement here. We have been around long enough to know that there are plenty of young people—probably hundreds—that don't fit the box we're about to throw them into. But so many of the ones we've met—our own kids and grandkids included—are lacking in a healthy respect for their elders and are much more likely to roll their eyes than those in other age groups.

So when we found one of them slouched in the porch swing, doing his best to swing himself off of the hooks and out into the lawn, there was a collective sigh and shaking of the head. Because the offender is a grandson of one of our residents, we will keep his identity a secret, but let it be known that the young man (we'll call him Ricky) was a shining example of what we dislike about this particular age group. He was twenty-two, his hair was four months past a trim, his left shoe was untied, and his shirt had a large, gaping hole in the arm pit that could be used as a second head-hole if the mood struck. He had a malnourished look to him common among those of his age and gender, who look to alcohol and cereal for sustenance. To look at him, you'd be hard pressed to guess when he had consumed his last vegetable. Years, perhaps. If someone tricked him into taking a multivitamin, he'd likely break out in hives.

No one was angrier with Ricky's presence than Robert, who had been occupying the porch swing from 6 a.m. until 8 a.m. for just about forever. When Robert saw an intruder from out one of the lobby windows, it was all he could do to keep from jumping up and down. What he did do was a lot of pointing and throwing his head around and asking Beverly, "What the—?" which was all he could manage, such was his exasperation.

Robert has been staging death scenes to rival those of Shakespeare on that porch swing every morning for more than twenty years, much to the delight of residents and visitors familiar with his act, and much to the horror and sometimes anger of those not in on the joke. Robert was, and is, a Last Stop staple. People expected him to be there. What were his fans going to think if he was suddenly absent? More than likely they would think that he had actually died and would be shocked and saddened unnecessarily.

This might be a good time to explain Robert's process. At a quarter to six, he saunters out to the porch swing and eats raisins until visitors start showing up. He then flops over and plays dead in the most dramatic fashion possible. First timers run over and yell for nurses and try to revive him, at which time he suddenly springs back to life and gushes over them for saving his life. Someone familiar with the act always says, "Come back tomorrow and you can save his life all over again." Others marvel at yet another original death expression, of which Robert seems to have an endless supply.

So you can understand his anxiety when it was almost six o'clock and he still wasn't at his post. If Ricky hadn't been wearing earphones, he might have heard Robert's faint cries of protest. And if he hadn't been a member of that particular age group that is prone to obliviousness to everything around them, he might have sensed it when Robert started jumping around and shaking his fist in the window behind him.

The only person in a position to help Robert with his predicament was Beverly, who first stated that her hands were tied and then held them up in front of her by way of demonstration, which was confusing and contradictory, and did nothing to help Robert's predicament or his mood.

She did suggest coaxing Holy Moses outside to scare the youth off the swing. Holy Moses rarely has to do much more than make an appearance to frighten the daylights out of people, so the suggestion had merit. The problem, of course, was getting Holy outside. For whatever reason, Holy has always been suspicious of Robert. Nobody knows what Holy's criterion is for us humans, but Robert is apparently lacking in some desirable qualities. Robert knew that anyone silly enough to try and manhandle him would learn a somewhat terrifying lesson. Robert himself had learned this a couple years ago when he grabbed Holy's collar and tried to lead him away from the buffet table. Holy is surprisingly agile for a dog his size, so when he suddenly knocked Robert down and began mauling him enthusiastically, it was all Robert could do to hang onto his bladder. Experiences of this kind tend to stay fresh in the mind.

Here we must clarify something, lest the reader get the wrong impression. Holy Moses in not mean. Even when he is mauling someone or something enthusiastically, he never inflicts any real damage. The noises he makes suggest that you are about to be eaten, bones and all, but we think this is done mostly for his own amusement. The only person Holy has actually bitten was Helen Watson (Midnight's keeper, in case you've forgotten) when she attempted a hostile takeover of The Last Stop a couple years ago. Needless to say, she had it coming.

But back to the story. Upon hearing Beverly say his name, Holy wandered into the lobby and stood between them, looking from Beverly to Robert and back again. Robert took this opportunity to try a feeble, "Here boy!" but Holy heard the timidity in the request and laid down.

Outside, Ricky was having his own problems. What Robert didn't know was that, despite his nonchalance on the swing, Ricky was dealing with his own turmoil. His grandfather (we'll call him

Lucy because it's hysterical) is one of our most lovable residents, but he is a bit of a disciplinarian when it comes to his grandkids. He had also funded Ricky's college education. The reason Ricky was spending so much time on the porch swing instead of going inside was because he was trying to come up with a good way of telling his grandfather that he was dropping out of college to pursue a career as a race car driver.

Perhaps if Robert would have known the young man's predicament, he would have said, "Do you mind? If you're just going to sit there, please find another seat. You can listen to those things anywhere," with a little less contempt. Ricky responded as expected, rolling his eyes and waving Robert off with a fluttering of his fingers.

It was at precisely this moment that Robert heard a car pull into the drive and realized that visitors were starting to arrive. So he tried a different, more desperate approach. Grasping Ricky's left earphone, he pulled it back until it reached its maximum stretch, and then let it snap back onto Ricky's unsuspecting ear. He then began shoving Ricky and yelling, "Get off my swing!" in a voice much more high-pitched and frantic than he would have liked.

When the shoving failed to produce anything but stunned immobility, Robert flung himself on top of Ricky and became immediately motionless. He closed his eyes and let his tongue lull out the side of his mouth. Ricky surmised that Robert had died right there on top of him and began to scream and writhe and call for help.

A police officer had just arrived to visit his mother and came running when he heard all the commotion. Several other visitors were behind him.

"Get him off of me!" Ricky yelled. Robert remained stiff and motionless. The officer grasped Robert by the shoulders and flipped him over, suddenly recoiling. "This man is dead!" he said. Now that it was confirmed, Ricky began rattling off his favorite expletives.

"Get a nurse!" the officer yelled, and began compressing Robert's chest. Before the officer could perform mouth to mouth, Robert suddenly sprang to his feet and, grasping the officer by the shoulders, said, "Officer! You have saved my life!"

Ricky realized that he'd been part of some elaborate prank and began to laugh. If there is one desirable quality of someone Ricky's age it is their ability to recognize and appreciate a good joke. The policeman, however, was not amused. Officers of the law aren't partial to pranks, nor are they fond of feeling silly, so it took just a moment for him to retrieve his handcuffs, spin Robert around, and shackle him up. When Robert asked what he could possibly be being arrested for, the officer said simply, "I'll think of something."

THE LAST STOP BULLETIN

THE WEATHER FRONT

Well, don't we feel silly. We made such a big deal about the first snow, and it was all for not. That's what we get for listening to Colleen McDowell on channel 4. We heard a rumor that she doesn't even have a degree. But she's perky in more ways than one, so we guess that qualifies her for something, we're just not sure what. What we are sure of is that she was positive it was going to snow and we spent Halloween in flip flops. This morning she was talking about how this winter might be one of the mildest on record, so you might as well start stocking up on supplies now.

YOU OUGHT TO KNOW

Well, not that anyone is surprised, Holy Moses and Harry won the Halloween costume contest. If we had known what they were up to, we wouldn't have bothered. A homeless man is one thing, but a man dressed up as a homeless lunch lady, complete with filthy blue dress and hair net, walking a Holy Moses wearing a flannel jacket and matching hunting cap, is quite another. When we found out that it was partially inspired by Vladimir and Estragon from Samuel Beckett's play, *Waiting for Godot*, it was all over. All that was missing was the donkey.

ACCORDING TO ROGER

The results are in! It doesn't matter that only three of you participated in my Halloween poll. (Okay, Roger, we should have warned you that polls don't usually go over well. We might all be retired, but that doesn't mean we want to spend our free time filling out forms.) Two of you voted for Regan in *The Exorcist*, but since she's actually an innocent victim, I had to throw her out. The correct answer would have been, "Who is the demon that possessed Regan in *The Exorcist*, Alex?" The other vote was for Annie in *Misery*, but I can't very well allow her to win because then I'd be admitting that I'm scared of girls, which I'm mostly not. So Freddy wins! Sleep tight everyone, whu, hu, hu, hu!

NOTES FROM THE MAINTENANCE SHED

In case you haven't noticed, raking season is in full swing. Harry tried his new blower/vacuum thing-a-ma-poop, but all it did was cover him in leaf dust and make him angry, so he's back to raking all the leaves by hand. We suggested that he wait to rake until the last leaf has fallen, but he rolled his eyes and made us feel silly. We were just trying to help.

Holy Moses is out there with him right now, making sure he lays down right where Harry is trying to rake. Harry doesn't seem to mind, though. More than once we've spotted them wrestling around in the leaf piles like a couple of kids. If it wasn't for Holy Moses, Harry would go completely bonkers this time of year.

You can all do your part by refraining from cutting through parts of the lawn that haven't been raked. Whole leaves are hard enough to rake, but leaves that have been stomped into little bits are nearly impossible.

KELLY'S CORNER

Kelly warned us to never use the word "Ole" in her column again if we know what's good for us. We were just trying to lighten things up, but we understand. When we have fun in her column it undermines her point. Anyone else notice that Kelly seems angrier than usual?

THE HOT SEAT

Technically he's done nothing wrong, but we've decided to put Mr. Bentley in the hot seat on principle. We know that our transport driver, Randy, sometimes drives faster than you are accustomed to, but that doesn't necessarily mean he isn't being safe. We would argue that driving too slow is just as dangerous as driving too fast.

Mr. Bentley, Randy is not without feelings, so when he sees you getting into a cab every time you need to go to the store, he can't help but be hurt. We know this was brought on by the near miss on the way to the casinos, but it wasn't his fault. When you're driving in a canyon, rocks sometimes fall onto the highway. When this happens, sometimes the bus driver has to swerve wildly and skirt the edge of the road where the drop off goes twenty feet down into the river. Just because you didn't see the rock, doesn't mean it didn't exist. If you don't want to go to the casinos anymore, we understand, but refusing to go on the fifteen minute round-trip to the grocery store seems a bit irrational.

GUEST COLUMN

The absence of a guest column this week can only be attributed to one thing: you are trying to come up with a way to top *The Giggling Green Goblin*. Don't. It isn't necessary to tell an entire story. Just tell us what's on your mind. Tell us what you're grateful for. Tell us about the book you're reading. Tell us anything, just as long as it's interesting to the community as a whole.

THE SUGGESTION BOX

You have spoken and we have listened, but we will not be adding energy drinks to the vending machines. If you need to get your buzz on, do it the old fashioned way and brew yourself a steaming cup of coffee. We know there are a few of you that have taken to the energy drink craze. We can tell by your incessant rocking and the way your eyes are always dilated.

HOLY MOSES!

There has been a recent trend of coming up with cute and clever names for Holy Moses. Please stop. Our fear is that Holy will become confused and will take his hostility out on innocent people. Here are some of the ones we've heard: Mr. Moses, Holy Who, which sounds more like Holy Whooooo, Turd Butt, which is offensive because Holy prides himself on keeping free of danglers, and Bubba-loni, which is clever, but not helping things. It's getting to the point where any time anyone says anything, Holy looks around just in case they're addressing him. This must be exhausting. It might seem petty, but we're just looking out for our little Pumpkin Head.

WINTER

The Last Stop Bulletin

The Weather Front

We were reading a quote today about how sunshine is delicious and how rain is refreshing, which is all well and good, but when it went on to talk about how snow is exhilarating and how the wind "braces us for the future," we felt we must cry foul. The fact that we have both snow and wind today makes us want to write a letter to the author. It makes us want to write a letter to the weather people, too, who promised us "unseasonably warm temperatures." Yes, we know, it's winter, but still . . .

You Ought to Know

This has to be one of our all time favorite "You Ought to Know" columns. We're so excited, we can hardly contain ourselves, so . . . we're going to stall for a while . . . write some random things . . . just to annoy you . . . string you along in the worst way . . . none of you better be skipping to the good stuff . . . that would deny us the immense pleasure we're feeling right now for holding out . . . happiness is having something to look forward to . . . good things come to those who . . .

Now we're on our own nerves.

You all remember Violet, the gorgeous Newfoundland whom Holy had one amazing summer with, but who tragically moved away some time ago? Well, she's going to come back and spend Christmas day with us! It turns out that Gloria and Todd are currently feuding with their respective families, so they've decided to ditch them and spend the day with us. Isn't that sweet?

You all know how much Holy likes Christmas, mostly because of the cheese trays, so imagine his reaction when Violet walks in wearing a big red bow! It ought to be a sight. Don't tell him, though. We know how weird that must sound, but this is Holy Moses we're talking about.

ACCORDING TO ROGER

Is it just me or has there been a surge in women residents lately? (Yes. First we will take over The Last Stop. Then we will take over the world!) They are gathering the troops. I have already been receiving hate mail and I can't figure out why. All they say is, "Go away!" or "Drop dead!" or "Who do you think you are?" to which I replied, "I think I'm Roger. Who else would I be?" If you're going to send me hate mail, please try to be specific about what you're angry about. I looked back at my columns and I just can't figure out what's so offensive. Is it just me or are women just so darned emotional? (Read that last sentence five times for clues.)

NOTES FROM THE MAINTENANCE SHED

Harry is going on vacation! Well, now it's weird because it's like we're all excited that Harry won't be here, which is certainly not the case. We're excited for him because he's been here for ten years and has never taken more than a few days off at any one time. And what's more impressive is that Harry has only missed one day of work due to illness since he's been here, and that was the day his appendix burst. Harry once said that he would like to dig the hole he's buried in. A bit morbid, perhaps, but it speaks volumes about his work ethic.

KELLY'S CORNER

While we wouldn't call today's note polite, it was absent of the overt hostility usually accompanying it. We're not sure if she's serious or not, but we figured we'd pass it along just to be safe. The note simply said, "You can walk in snow if you have snow shoes." We don't know if she's planning on ordering snow shoes, or if she expects you to provide them, or if she's just annoyed that more of you don't make use of the trails during the colder months. We have a feeling it's a combination of all three.

THE HOT SEAT

Here we are again for the third time this year. While it pains us to admit it, we are now officially hypocrites. We went on a bit of a rant about energy drinks a couple weeks ago with never having had the pleasure of trying one. While they don't taste very good, the focus and energy they give us has us looking forward to trying all the various brands. We are now officially full of zip!

GUEST COLUMN

I want to publicly apologize to Ms. B.A. Fisher, whom I mistakenly hit in the head with a snowball. I swear, I thought it was my wife. Why do you think I threw it so hard?

I was told that Ms. Fisher's initials stand for Bad Ass, and that I should sleep with one eye open. I'm taking this seriously.

It has just occurred to me that my wife reads the bulletin. Please, Ms. Bad Ass, don't disclose my identity. I'm sure what you come up with will be punishment o-plenty without getting my wife involved.

Forever sorry,

Anonymous
Room 35, Buena Vista Wing

THE SUGGESTION BOX

You have spoken, but we have decided not to listen, partially because it addresses us personally, and what it suggests we stop doing is entirely too much fun to give up. The suggestion that kept coming up was a plea that we stop interrupting the "According to Roger" column with parenthetic, humorous comments aimed at undermining Roger's opinion.

First of all, we are the publishers of this rag, so if we find an opinion that we don't agree with, we feel it's our duty to bring attention to it, and if it's done in an amusing way, so much the better.

You know, Roger, if we find out it was you that riddled the suggestion box with this type of stuff, things can only get worse. If you know what's good for you, you'll let us go on humoring ourselves in peace.

HOLY MOSES!

Just when we think we've seen it all, Holy Moses reminds us that we will never have seen it all as long as he is alive. This morning, Beverly caught Mr. Moses trying to go number two in Midnight's litter box.

In a way, it's not that surprising. Holy isn't a fan of snow, especially if it's blowing, so it just might have been a clever solution to a problem. But knowing him the way we do, it's more likely that he did it in retaliation for the way Midnight mocks him from her basking spots. The fact that it also alleviated his need to go outside in the snow was probably just icing on the cake. We're just thankful that he couldn't manage to get all four feet in the box, or he probably would have gone through with it.

We hope this isn't the start of a feud. If Holy and Midnight start trying to one-up each other, it's only a matter of time before the whole building comes tumbling down.

EVERYTHING IS ACCUMULATIVE

Stanley Junior High held a contest over the long Christmas vacation for their seventh and eighth graders. Their task was to interview someone who had changed their life through diet and exercise. A seventh grader named Tiffany Wilcox decided to forgo the obvious and skip the relatives and family friends and seek out a complete stranger, which is what brought her to us, and is why we set her up with Walter Peabody.

First a disclaimer: most of the stories in this little book of ours are purely for entertainment, but occasionally something happens or something is said that has the ability to teach and to inspire and excluding it because it isn't full of knee slappers wouldn't be right.

Most of you know Walter, but the rest of the world hasn't had the pleasure. Walter is just one more example of the amazing assemblage of oldish people we have here. Yes, this is a slight departure from our usual snarky, sarcastic selves, but we can be sentimental and sweet when we want to be, so shut up.

What follows is the full transcript of that interview. You will likely notice that Tiffany doesn't make an appearance. This isn't because we edited her out, it's because she literally didn't say anything.

WALTER: "Do you mind if we walk? I used to drink soda like that, three or four a day. You're young, so you can get away with it. I was two hundred and eighty-five pounds at my heaviest. That was three years ago. And now look at me! How much do you think I weigh? I woke up this morning weighing one hundred and forty-eight pounds.

"I weigh myself most mornings. It makes me feel good about things; starts the day off on the right foot. I certainly don't recommend living in the past, but the occasional look back to see how far you've come is a good thing.

"Hold on a second. I need to start my stopwatch. This is how it all started. This path, this stopwatch. When you're exercising it has to be measurable so you know you're getting better. The weight comes off slowly, so you have to find other ways to track your progress.

"This path is exactly one mile. I'm going to go around three times, but don't worry, you don't have to do the whole three miles if you don't want to. I'm going to have to move fast, though, because I have to beat my last time of fifty-three minutes and twenty-eight seconds. I try to beat my time by five seconds each time I do it. You look like you'll be able to keep up.

"It's funny how things work out. I didn't start caring about my health until I was seventy-two years old. I figured I had all the time in the world. Time does run out, though. Eventually it all catches up with us. Interesting how the closer it gets, the less I think about it.

"I don't stay healthy to live longer, necessarily. I stay healthy so I can enjoy the time I have left. You have to enjoy your life. It seems we get so busy we forget that sometimes. Even when we're not busy we forget that. People go on vacation and forget that. Hawaii, Disney Land! There they are, riding the roller coaster and they're thinking about something they have to deal with when they get back.

"You want to know one of the best pieces of advice I ever received? Never think about anything unless you are prepared and able to do something about it in that moment. You'd be amazed how that frees up your mind. Work, school, all that stuff that exists out in front of you, take it as it comes. If you've done your homework and you've studied, then you've done all you can do. They say that all anxiety stems from a feeling of unpreparedness. There's something profound in that. It means that you can handle anything with enough preparation. I'll give you an example. If you're scared to death because of a speech you have to give in front of the class, first do it twenty times in front of the mirror, then do it twenty times for your family, and then do it in front of a group of friends. Do it so often that when you get up there you don't have to think about what you're doing.

"One other thing: don't accept things. Don't ever say, 'that's just the way it is,' or 'that's just the way I am.' You can always improve yourself and your life. You can always get better at things. You know how I know? Three years ago I came out here to walk this path for the first time and I had to stop every hundred feet or so. I never forget that. I smile every time I go up this hill we're coming up to. I stood in front of that hill for probably ten minutes the first time, just staring at it, looking for a way around it, wanting more than anything to turn back. But I didn't. I just started walking. And that's what you have to do. Emerson said, 'Do the thing and you'll have the power,' so I just put one foot in front of the other and got on with it.

"I can say all this now, but when I first came to live here, I was a real mess, and not just physically. I had spent my whole life looking forward to the day when I didn't have to be anywhere or do anything. It's a terrible thing to wake up one morning and realize you've had it wrong. It's a trap: constantly waiting for some future event to make you happy. Waiting for five o'clock so you can leave the job you don't like, waiting for the weekend, waiting for vacation, waiting for the bell to ring so you can meet your friends, waiting for retirement. That's what I did. Thirty, forty, fifty years from now, that's when I'll be really happy! That's not living, that's waiting.

"You see this? This is the notebook I record all my times in. I've gone through three of these. I don't throw them away. They mean too much. It's my journey. It's all right here in these pages. I started with one lap. I timed it. The next time I walked, my goal was to beat my time, even if it was only by one second. I walked three days a week, and then four, and then five. I walk every day now, unless the weather is really bad. I enjoy it. When it got to the point where I couldn't beat my time without jogging, I started wearing weights on my ankles and started the whole process over again. When that got to be too easy, I increased the distance. You always have to change things. Your body will adapt to anything if you do it long enough. You have to set little challenges for yourself. It gives you a purpose. The stopwatch gives you something to worry about other than the fact that you're tired. Consistent, steady progress, that's how I did it.

"Everything is accumulative. This idea that you have to put in this massive effort to get results is what holds most people back. I'll tell you this: doing some physical activity twenty minutes a day, every day, is light years better than killing yourself for two hours once a week. Effort is accumulative. Everything is accumulative. All these big, cataclysmic events we like to say took us by surprise are actually just all the little things adding up. You didn't fail the test because the test was too hard, or the teacher was unfair, or you woke up late. You failed the test because of all the nights you spent talking on the phone instead of studying. People don't wake up one morning broke and in debt any more than they wake up one morning overweight and sick. Two or three sodas, no big deal. Two or three sodas a day over the course of a life . . . they add up.

"Of course, it works the other way, too. You'd be surprised how something small done consistently can completely alter your life. Start saving five dollars a day until you don't think about it anymore and see what happens. Replace sodas with unsweetened iced tea and see how much better you feel after a month. The trick is to find the little things that make the biggest difference.

"Most people don't get in shape because it's easier not to. It really is that simple. If you don't have a good enough reason for doing something, it's just easier not to do it. There are all sorts of reasons. Sometimes the thought of fitting into a favorite pair of pants is enough to get you going. Sometimes it takes a doctor telling you that you'll be dead in a year if you don't lose the weight. Whatever the reason, the perceived reward has to be greater than the perceived discomfort. You see how that works?

"It doesn't have to be dramatic. There's something to be said about getting really tired and deciding that you deserve something better. That's how it was with me. I finally took an honest look at my life. I gave up the stories about why my life was the way it was. There was no more hiding. I finally saw all the behaviors and habits for what they were.

"There's usually a trigger. For me, it was buying a pair of slip-on shoes so I wouldn't have to go through all the trouble of tying them. You might laugh, but when your belly was as big as mine, it was a real chore. Instead of fixing the real problem, I found a way around it. I was an avoider in the worst way. I worked around things. I shoved everything in the closet, or under the bed, or hid it behind baggy clothes. All the emotional stuff, the self-loathing and bitterness that came with it, that got hidden away, too.

"That's why walking is so therapeutic. It gives you the time and space to work through things.

"I'll tell you one more thing, and then I'll let you be on your way. We're coming back around now. Just over that hill is where we started. What I want to say is this: I used to go through this ritual every Sunday night. 'This week's going to be different. This is the week I will change my life.' I did the same thing with New Years. I used to start planning all my resolutions clear back in November because it made me feel good. It's fun to plan, but it isn't effective unless you actually do something. There is something magical that takes place when you do something the minute you get inspired to do it. You think, 'I really should start eating better,' and you immediately go clean all the crap out of your refrigerator. You think, 'I should exercise more,' and you put your shoes on and walk around the block.

"So remember this, my dear: Monday is no different than Wednesday, and January 1st is no different than June 8th. If you want to change your life, put one foot in front of the other and get on with it. And above all else, enjoy your life."

THE LAST STOP BULLETIN

THE WEATHER FRONT

It's going to be a holly jolly Christmas! The good people on the Weather Channel (not the news) have assured us that we're going to get a good helping of the white stuff just in time for Christmas. We might spend a lot of time complaining about snow, but when there's a fire roaring in the fireplace and *Deck the Halls* playing softly in the background, you really can't beat it. Ms. Theron passing around the whiskey bottle helps, too!

YOU OUGHT TO KNOW

The community Christmas tree is something to see. Your creative decorating is overwhelming. However, we wouldn't be the Chin-wags if we didn't point out that some of you went a bit overboard with the garland, which is so thick in places that you can't see the twinkling lights, and what is a Christmas tree without twinkling lights?

Keep in mind that Midnight has taken to spending the majority of her time sleeping beneath the tree, so be cautious when adding ornaments. She's pretty mild mannered these days, but if you startle her, who knows how she'll react.

The theater will be showing all classic Christmas movies this week. And by "classic" we don't necessarily mean black and white. Despite what some of you think, there are movies other than *It's a Wonderful Life* that fit the bill.

ACCORDING TO ROGER

HO HO HO! Yours truly will be playing the part of Santa Clause this year, so if there's anything you really want, come sit on my lap and tell me about it! (Completely inappropriate.) If anyone has a pair of black boots, size ten, please let me know. I got rid of my only pair last year. Also, if you wouldn't mind reminding the grandchildren that Santa doesn't like having his beard tugged on, I'd appreciate it. (Big baby.)

NOTES FROM THE MAINTENANCE SHED

Don't pay attention to all the racket, Harry is just finishing up the last of the decorations. This is Harry's favorite time of year, so if you hear excessive whistling and humming, that'll be why. Of course, it might just be the eggnog he starts drinking in bulk this time of year. Anyway, he's really outdone himself with all the lights he added out front. It almost looks like we were plucked out of a Thomas Kinkade painting.

KELLY'S CORNER

Please no caroling in the gym, it's distracting. (The 'please' is ours.) And just because Kelly is wearing a Santa hat in the gym doesn't mean it's all right for you to wear one. She must be in a good mood, though, because she wanted us to mention that you all are rocking it. We're going to assume that's a complement.

THE HOT SEAT

Okay, there can only be one Christmas angel, and currently we have three jockeying for position. There were four, but one of them mysteriously showed up in the trashcan. Whoever is partaking in this sort of ornament sabotage should try to remember the meaning of Christmas. In an attempt to settle things with as little violence as possible, we will take a vote to decide which one gets top billing. Beverly is drawing up the ballots. They should be ready this afternoon.

GUEST COLUMN

I want to say once and for all that I forgive my parents for not getting me the Schwinn Model BA-107 Standard Auto-cycle for Christmas, 1946, when I was 10, even though Joan Crawford herself recommended it.

Whew! That feels better. I'd been hanging onto that one for a long time!

--Mr. James Baker

THE SUGGESTION BOX

You have spoken and we have listened. While we like the idea of having a White Elephant gift exchange, you have to keep in mind that there are a hundred and fifty residents at our little abode. We'd have to start it on Halloween in order to be done by Christmas.

HOLY MOSES!

Christmas came early for Holy Moses. Gloria and Todd mended their relationship with their parents and decided it was only right that they spend Christmas day with them, but they didn't want to disappoint us, so they came three days early. To honor the occasion, we let Holy open one of his presents early.

He loved his new collar with the snowmen and bells on it so much that when Violet came over to take a better look at it, he snapped at her. It didn't escalate, though, because Holy immediately rolled over and pawed at her apologetically. Ever since Violet bit off a chunk of his ear, they've had a complicated relationship. Holy holds grudges. We've known this for years. And it appears he isn't entirely ready to let her off the hook. It probably didn't help that many of you were showering Violet with the affection you'd normally reserve for Holy Moses.

Even though their meeting wasn't the raving success we had hoped for, they did share a moment or two. Perhaps if there weren't so many distractions they could work things out.

Now back to the collar . . . Did we mention that it has bells on it? We thought this would be safe because of Holy's relative inactivity, but apparently the jingling has inspired him to run up and down the hallways, whipping his head around until he gets dizzy and has to sit down. We hope this is temporary.

Midnight loves it almost as much as he does. She has taken to stalking the collar and then swatting the bells furiously when Holy isn't looking. Strangely, Holy doesn't seem to mind. For now, all is well in the animal kingdom.

Up in Flames

Holidays around here are pretty eventful, but last year, we must say, took the cake. While a belief in Santa Clause has diminished over the years, a love for Christmas caroling has only grown stronger. If we could get away with it (which, of course, we could, but it would be weird, even for us) we would carol all year-round.

It usually begins around October. We start hearing the normal hallway and restaurant chatter interrupted by random Christmas songs being partially hummed. We do love our holiday music, but it's not always Christmas music that catches our fancy. Back in November, little Ms. Laverty went around humming the *Halloween* theme song, alternating between the high notes and the bass notes with alarming accuracy. It still gives us chills.

It wasn't her fault. The poor thing had never seen the movies, so she had no idea what havoc she was causing. Her great grandson had learned to play the song on the keyboard for a Halloween-themed social at his school. Every time he visited her, he'd plop down in front of the keyboard she keeps in her spare room and play it over and over again, so it's not surprising that it stuck in her head.

Of course, no one knew any of this. We just assumed that she had been temporarily possessed by Michael Myers and patiently waited for her good nature to prevail, but it didn't stop until she suggested that the choir add it to their repartee and Mr. Jenson led her by her gloved hand down to the theater and showed her why that might not be a good idea. She did quite a bit of screaming and told him the whole story. This year, Ms. Laverty is spending Halloween in her room, playing solitaire and watching *Elf.*

Now back to Christmas.

The choir rehearses all year for the Christmas Eve recital. It apparently takes this long to learn how to sing *Away in a Manger* in alternating keys . . .

Everything went as expected until *Silent Night.* Because it's the closer, we thought it would be nice if everyone held a lit candle emotionally over their heads. Why we felt this was necessary, we don't remember, but because of the expense of candles, and the hassle of getting everyone together, we didn't want to rehearse this little maneuver.

Harry had warned us that we should allow more space between rows to give the fire more room, but we scoffed at him, shooed him away, and called him silly. We did this because we assumed that everyone would be capable of lighting their candles without, in-turn, lighting the hair of the person standing in front of them. We were wrong. Some of the blame can be placed on the candles themselves. We bought the big red ones because they looked like Christmas. If we would have looked at the packaging closer, we would have learned that these particular candles produce a flame twice the size of normal candles. As you can see, it was kind of a perfect storm, only with fire.

In the end, it was our fault and we take full responsibility. We've looked around for someone else to blame, but it keeps coming back to us. Normally we would just place ourselves in the hot seat and be done with it, but because six different people in different parts of the auditorium had their hair set on fire, we felt it warranted the longer version. For the record, we apologize profusely, and you know we're sincere because we don't do anything profusely.

We wish we could say that the fire was the only concern, but some unknown person, apparently sleeping during fire safety class, yelled, "Fire!" and panic ensued, during which several people were trampled. We're just lucky that none of you weigh enough to do any real damage and no one was seriously hurt.

What we don't feel responsible for is the fact that most of you dropped your candles before extinguishing them, thus adding to the potential magnitude of the fire. Yes, we realize that there wouldn't have been candles to drop if there hadn't been candles in the first place, but we feel this was a poor response to an already dangerous situation. The fact that the whole building didn't go up in smoke is a Christmas miracle.

All in all, Ms. Wilma Benny, Frank Cather, Ava Hall, and Mr. and Mrs. Willis all have slightly new hairstyles. Let us be the first to say that you all look marvelous!

We failed to mention Nurse Missy. While the others were left with at least some remnants of their hair, Missy's hair and eyebrows went up so fast due to all the flammable hair products she uses that none of it could be saved. We're just glad that Ernie had the presence of mind to tackle her and smother her head with his body before the flames could do any real damage. As a happy side note, this little act of bravery has done wonders for Ernie's personality. He now wears sunglasses indoors.

Missy, on the other hand, took a leave of absence and required counseling. We're happy to report that her and her curly locks are back in full swing. She has started wearing fireproof head-wear during events, though, so the memories must linger.

On a happy note, the wig Ava wore while her hair was growing back was such a hit that she adopted it as her permanent look. Shaving her head regularly, she says, is a hassle, but all the complements she gets makes it worth it.

The real hero of the day, not surprisingly, was Harry. He was a regular one man fire brigade. The multiple fires were no match for Harry and his backpack-mounted fire extinguishers.

Holy Moses, for those of you wondering why he didn't at least play a supporting role in such a significant event, was sleeping peacefully under Beverly's desk. Holy loves Christmas, but he dislikes caroling. Most of the songs are so upbeat and optimistic that he expects treats to come his way, and when this doesn't happen, he gets annoyed. Also, the volume and intensity at which the songs are sung probably hurts his ears.

The Last Stop Bulletin

The Weather Front

For all our complaining about the colder months, leave it to Colorado weather to put us squarely in our place. We've tried to put a gloomy spin on things, but the fact is that the weather this morning, winter or otherwise, couldn't be more perfect: sixty-six degrees, not a cloud in the sky, and a gentle breeze swaying all the naked trees.

You Ought to Know

It's that time of year again. No, we're not going to go on another rant. Actually, it's just the opposite. We had forgotten that this is the time of year that Chef Amato starts adding his famous chili to the menu. Just remember that he doesn't write down any of his recipes so it might take him a batch or two to get it just right.

ACCORDING TO ROGER

We are men, here us roar! (Oh, please!) Yes, it was I that filled the suggestion box with my grievances towards the Chin-wags. Because that got no response, I want to go on the record by stating that I find it inappropriate and rude how the Chin-wags keep inserting sarcastic comments in the middle of my column. They're trying to force me out, but, fear not, I will push on. Perhaps they will eventually tire of this childish behavior. (Never. It's hysterical.)

On with today's topic, which I fear is quite depressing. Those of you who had high hopes for our Denver Broncos going to the Super Bowl this year, well, it's not going to happen. There's always next year, though! (And the one after that, and the one after that . . .)

NOTES FROM THE MAINTENANCE SHED

He's Baaaaaaaack! And look at him, all tan and plump from his trip to Steamboat. He tells us that it's actually wind burn, and the bloat is from excessive salt intake, but never mind all that!

No one was happier to see him than Holy Moses, who was so excited that he raced outside and peed on Mr. Gallager's leg. We apologize, Mr. Gallager. We're sure it wasn't personal, you just happened to be the closest vertical surface.

Thanks to everyone that went out of their way yesterday to get the place sparkling for Harry's return. Let's try to keep it that way. Now that he's rested, he's not likely to miss anything. Harry loved the "WELCOME BACK" banner, though he was obviously concerned about what was used to attach it to the building. We saw him earlier heading that way with a can of paint, but don't worry, he was whistling, which is nice and disconcerting all at the same time.

KELLY'S CORNER

This is the note we found stapled to our door this morning: "Kettle Bells, people! Bells! Not balls. Kettle Bells!" We have no idea what she's talking about, but when she staples something to your door it's usually best to pass it along. Apparently, you all offended the kettle bells by calling them balls . . . We're going to assume that at least a few of you know what she's talking about.

GUEST COLUMN

Hi all! Just wanted to give a big shout-out to my grand kid, Keller, for getting an A on his math quiz. Good for you kid!

THE HOT SEAT

No explanation needed, but we'll say it anyway. What are the chances that his grandkid reads The Last Stop Bulletin? Please, no public service announcements or "shout-outs." While we applaud Keller on his math quiz, we doubt this is of much interest to the casual reader. (Yes, we realize that today's bulletin is out of order, but it works better this way.)

THE SUGGESTION BOX

You have spoken and we have listened. We don't know why we're agreeing to this considering our personal views on movie sequels that don't know when to quit, but we are agreeing to a marathon showing of all the Rocky movies this coming Tuesday.

We don't know why the sudden interest, but since we just wrapped up our month-long "romantic comedies that also make us cry" series, we figure it was only fair. We aren't sure who keeps suggesting the Rocky movies, but perhaps someone will appear jogging the halls in stained sweat pants and the mystery will be solved.

For all the women cursing us right now, we'll state our case: the first Rocky movie, you must admit, is a pretty darned good movie, though admittedly gory at the end. The second and third are tolerable. After that it's pretty rough going. If it wasn't for the recent Rocky Balboa movie that came out a couple years ago to end it all on a high note, we probably wouldn't be considering doing this. If you still feel the need to complain, we gently remind you that it's a Tuesday, for crying out loud, find something else to do.

So, on that note, "Adriaaaaan!"

HOLY MOSES!

In reference to today's "You Ought to Know" column, we want to remind everyone that Holy Moses likes chili just as much as the rest of us, so unless you want the facility to smell like a napalm bomb went off, be strong when he comes looking for handouts.

YOU CAN'T KEEP A GOOD MAN DOWN

A lot of visitors have been remarking lately about what an upbeat, fun place we have here, which is all true, but what most of you probably don't know is that it wasn't always this way. We don't mean to say that we were all a bunch of curmudgeons, but twenty years ago we were much more average in our behaviors: quick to criticize, quick to judge, slow to forgive, and much more prone to mood swings and crankiness. And that got us thinking about Archie, who we lost earlier this year at the ripe old age of ninety-seven, and how big a part he played in the formation of our collective better selves.

While Archie was universally loved in the end, when he arrived in 1995, he had it pretty rough. It was just bad timing that he had the song *Ding Dong the Witch is Dead* in his head just after moving in. Anyone who has had that particular song in their head knows how hard it is to remove once it has taken root. It could happen to anyone. But first impressions being what they are, it isn't surprising that Archie wasn't welcomed with open arms. There is no telling how many times he had mumbled, hummed, or sung that particular song in the first few weeks he was here, and there is no telling how many silent death threats were vowed by those close enough to hear it for the eight millionth time.

Archie, god love him, even without the offensive song, was afflicted with a personality trait that generally brings out the worst in people. It's a weird sort of paradox. Archie had an uncanny ability to shrug off the worst life had to offer. Nothing got to him. And he had so much good cheer left over that he went looking for people in need of a human pick-me-up. But instead of being cheered up, they often took a turn for the worse.

It was surprising just how universal this was. Young and old alike were inspired to use filthy language. Even small children, not old enough to be annoyed by anything other than a lack of food or sleep, would suddenly clench their little fists when Archie entered the room. And if he approached them with baby talk, they would shriek and writhe and try to sound out obscenities.

The real tragedy with Archie was that he was genuinely trying to help. We feel terrible, because while it's easy to point out other people's inappropriate behavior, it's not quite as cozy admitting to our own. But we were as guilty as anyone. We didn't have a hot seat back then, but if we had, Archie probably would have been a regular recipient.

What we've learned from all this is that people aren't interested in being cheered up. What they're after, more often than not, is sympathy. For some reason we all seem to be comforted by the complaints and tragedies of others. People with problems empathize with other people with problems. When we complain, we're not looking for a solution. We're looking for someone to say, "Oh my god! That's awful. You poor thing!" Archie's over-eagerness to fix everyone's problems seems to have been his downfall. Instead of nodding his head knowingly when someone told him of their latest catastrophe, Archie said things like, "Well, I guess you'll never do that again!" or "Tomorrow's another day," or "Well, at least you have a roof over your head!" There were times when Archie tried to complain, but he could never do it with a straight face and no one believed him.

To make matters worse, when Archie broke his ankle after tripping (or was he tripped?) down the stairs, he took what should have been a reason for complaint and turned it into something positive. Most of us would have been a constant choir of how unlucky we were. Archie, on the other hand, found that once he figured out the correct positioning of the crutches and the optimal angle with which to hold his injured foot, he could propel himself down the hallway with much less effort than it would have taken him by simply walking on two good legs. He was so excited by this that he started timing how long it took him to get from his room to various points in the building. And if that wasn't bad enough, he tried to get people to race him down the hallway. A few were suckered into this, only to be demoralized and reminded of their inadequacies. And when Archie asked them if they wanted to try the crutches, they turned red and mumbled ill wishes.

It didn't end there. When Archie noticed that the strength in his good leg had increased because of the added use, he decided to get a voluntary cast for the good leg once the other one healed, so it, too, could gain the benefits. This was almost too much. By hobbling up and down stairs on completely unnecessary crutches, he was inadvertently holding up everyone's weaknesses in front of them and dancing them around. There is nothing quite as annoying to the complainer than watching someone joyously embracing struggle. Some openly wished he'd broken both legs.

It wasn't long before Archie was completely shunned. When he tried to speak, he was interrupted or completely ignored. When he tried to insert himself into activities, the activity was abruptly stopped.

All of this open hostility eventually wore Archie down. By Christmas morning of his first year, he had had enough. What exactly it was that triggered the change, we don't know. We should have seen it coming, though. Looking back, the whole week before Christmas, the smile that seemed a permanent fixture on his face had begun to droop at the edges. The twinkle in his eye was still there, but it had dimmed considerably, and he walked with slumped shoulders.

The first sign that something was really wrong was when Archie snapped at the server for forgetting the cream for his coffee. Tracy was so confused by the out of character tone with which he spoke to her, that she laughed and then dropped the tray of drinks she was carrying. This momentarily snapped Archie out of it, but after helping her clean it up, he slumped back in the booth and picked at his eggs and toast before getting up and leaving without leaving a tip.

Next we found him sitting in the lobby next to the Christmas tree, listlessly flicking the ornaments. And when one dropped and broke, instead of gathering it up and going out to find a suitable replacement, he clucked his tongue and flicked another one. And when that one fell and broke, he laughed and clapped. The Santa hat on his head only made the scene more disturbing.

Later that afternoon, when the choir came into the restaurant for a bit of unexpected caroling, Archie was seen rubbing his temples. And when Ms. Ross came in pulling a miniature Rudolf on wheels behind her, singing *Grandma Got Run Over by a Reindeer,* Archie stood up abruptly, tossed his Santa hat on the ground, stomped on it, and then tackled Rudolf.

All of this he did in complete silence, but after a handful of residents pulled him off of Rudolf, he banged both fists on the nearest table and yelled something indecipherable. Some said it sounded like, "You suck!" but we think it was more likely just a primal scream, void of any actual language, just years of frustrations held in, suddenly being violently sent forth into the world. We figured Archie had spent so much time finding the good that all the bad stuff he was ignoring backed up on him, eventually wearing him down until the inevitable result being the mauling of a perfectly innocent reindeer.

The next place we found Archie was on the porch swing with his face buried in his hands.

And then a funny thing happened. Everyone who had witnessed the restaurant scene began filing out the front doors, and when they saw Archie, they cheered and draped their arms around him and offered to make him a strong drink to help calm him. And they laughed and told him stories about the time they melted down and how what he had done wasn't as bad as that, and they laughed and embraced him because he was one of them after all.

The story might have ended there, but what no one knew until years later was that Archie's meltdown had been a complete ruse; a carefully planned, meticulously executed series of events aimed at infiltrating and ultimately influencing his fellow residents. Only this time he took a different approach. He decided that other people's problems weren't his responsibility. He couldn't tell people how to live their lives. All he could do was be himself and hope that some of his positive energy rubbed off on them.

And it did. Soon Betty, who was pleasant to those she knew, but standoffish to people she didn't, started smiling and greeting everyone by their first names, and Jimmie from the Buena Vista wing, began putting his arm around people and giving them a good shake, just like Archie. Others followed. Like Walter Peabody said, "Everything is accumulative." Smiles add up.

THE LAST STOP BULLETIN

THE WEATHER FRONT

Longfellow once said that the best thing to do when it's raining is to let it rain. We're quite sure he was using rain as a metaphor, but today we must take it literal, though with slight alterations: When the snow is whipping around at 40 mph, the only thing to do is let the snow whip around at 40 mph. Not quite as poetic as Mr. Longfellow, but what else is there to do?

We just happened to be watching the news when we wrote the above, which has now inspired us to change our tone from one of bitterness to one of gratitude. If we were unfortunate enough to live in Buffalo, we'd be waking up to nearly three feet of snow this morning. With that in mind, the ten inches we piled up over night is really quite pretty.

YOU OUGHT TO KNOW

You've probably noticed that the library is so full that the books are starting to spill out into the hallway. And now that Ms. Patterson's contact down at the library has agreed to give us all the books they don't sell at their annual sale, we need to come up with some creative ways to expand our library without actually knocking down walls. As it is, the books are shelved three deep, which seems to defeat the purpose of having more books.

ACCORDING TO ROGER

Don't fall for it! The Rocky movie marathon was just the Chin-wags way of trying to appease us. However, now that I think about it, it was pretty generous of them to dedicate a full day to manly movies. Perhaps they're turning the corner. I will still say what I was going to say, but to show my appreciation, I will no longer put it in all CAPS: rise up and give the Chin-wags what for. (Silly man.)

NOTES FROM THE MAINTENANCE SHED

Well, this is a first. Harry doesn't particularly like snow, but he always puts that to one side and does the necessary shoveling and plowing in earnest. However, this morning he's been standing in the lobby drinking coffee and staring out at the falling snow with a little smile on his gruff face. What this all means is anyone's guess, but you might want to dig out the moon boots just in case the walks aren't clear . . .

This just in: Harry pointed out that the wind is doing the necessary shoveling for him by piling it up against vertical surfaces. That mystery is now solved.

KELLY'S CORNER

The most anxious part of our day is always when we first arrive. It doesn't matter how early we get in, Kelly always has her grievances stuck to the door. So imagine our surprise when we found a cute little card with an elephant on it stapled to our door. Inside the card were the words, "Here's to getting better."

We're not sure what's going on here. Perhaps she was drugged. Perhaps someone snatched the real message and replaced it with the card. We'll never know because we don't want to ask her about it. If she did leave the card, we won't be able to hide our shock, and if she didn't leave the card, she'll knock the whole place down trying to find out who did. So, "Here's to getting better!" We just don't know what that has to do with elephants.

THE HOT SEAT

This week's hot seat goes to "Anonymous," who submitted the following in hopes that it would appear in the guest column:

The gloom in the night oppresses me uncomfortably in the sheets that surround me. Go, I must, into the black to find the sliver that fails to light. But, uncomfortably, I return to the oppression and carry on, though I wish it not so. -- Anonymous

Okay, the guest column isn't supposed to be used for poetry or whatever the heck that was. We're sorry to have subjected you to such depressing material, but we were so surprised that we had a raving lunatic in our midst, that we felt inclined to at least include it here. Bravo, Anonymous, your work has officially been published, but in the future try not to be so darned gloomy. Who in the heck wants to be oppressed uncomfortably anyway?

GUEST COLUMN

In the spirit of the Holidays, I think we should all do our part in keeping the facility safe. I propose we start a shoveling crew to help Harry when the snow gets heavy.

(Great idea, but it'll never fly. Harry doesn't like complements, nor does he like help. If he accepts help, then he has to admit that he needed help. Your heart is in the right place, though. Maybe you can make him an appreciation cake or something instead.)

THE SUGGESTION BOX

You have spoken and we have listened. With the winter season rapidly coming to an end, some of you have expressed disappointment that we didn't make better use of the snow in the way of snowmen, snow angles, and forts. We'll politely remind you that there are warmer ways to recapture your youth, but the suggestion that we organize a Resident vs. Staff snowball fight isn't without some appeal.

HOLY MOSES!

Here's a problem we never anticipated. What with the forty-eight feet of snow we've gotten over the last several hours, mixed with the wind-chill factor of minus god knows what, our boy has decided that going to the bathroom outside is not something he's interested in doing. When we tried to get him out, he flopped over, and when we tried to get him back up, he started speaking in tongues.

After he calmed down, he came up with his own solution of sorts. When we opened the door again, he turned around and backed up his rear-end just far enough to clear the door and then proceeded to poop. If this was any other canine, perhaps we would have been surprised. Going on the front steps isn't much better than going in the middle of the lobby, so if this keeps up, we may have to fashion some sort of diaper for him.

SPRING

The Last Stop Bulletin

The Weather Front

Ah, spring has sprung! Finally! Out with the old and in with the new! The fact that we are having decidedly un-spring-like weather this morning isn't even fazing us. The calendar tells us it's spring, so it is so. Yes, we get the occasional spring snow storm that buries cars and breaks tree limbs, but it's spring! Before you know it the grass will be a lush green and the flowers will start a-bloomin'. Tank tops and flip-flops, here we come! It'll take a few days to get the gloom out this week, but by Wednesday we're looking at mostly sunny skies with the highs hovering around sixty-eight degrees. In case you missed it: SPRING IS HERE!

You Ought to Know

Speaking of flowers a bloomin', this year we will be constructing a community garden down by the picnic area. Construction will begin as soon as the ground has thawed. By, "we," we mean Harry, of course, who will begin shoveling in earnest as soon as he's able. Once again we will suggest that he rent some sort of machinery to help with the digging and the hauling, but it'll probably go unheeded. Perhaps he likes all the physical labor. Perhaps it's more gratifying. We just hope that he pumped up the wheel on his wheel barrow. Harry has already drawn up some plans, but they're constantly changing. We don't know much yet, but he's been talking a lot about vegetables lately.

ACCORDING TO ROGER

It seems that our little rushing river is chock-a-block full of trout! Who knew? And if you did, you didn't bother telling me. I guess I always assumed there were fish, but it never occurred to me to do any fishing. It reminds me of fishing with my granddad . . . though, what I seem to remember most is how frustrated he'd get trying to untangle the fishing line, and how he'd eventually throw his tackle box into whatever body of water we were fishing in. (We'll overlook ending that sentence with a preposition this time, but don't make a habit out of it.)

But that was a long time ago, so I think it's high time I dig out the old fishing cap, vest, and waders and scurry on down and give it a try. A little bird told me that red and white daredevils worked well last year. I've got a Sportsman catalog if anyone wants to look at lures or pontoon boats. (Sounds riveting, but pontoon boats? Even we know you don't use a boat in a river.)

Also, as a side note, I've been doing a lot of reading lately about improving the quality of your life, so I'm going to start working some lessons into the column. This is not my stuff. I'm not Socrates. I am not a wise-man speaking to you from on high. I just thought I'd pass along some of the things I've learned.

NOTES FROM THE MAINTENANCE SHED

This is the time of year when Harry likes to get creative. Along with the community garden, he's also been drawing up plans for a water feature that would double as a wading pool. Last summer he dug out the hill behind the fitness center to make a cool-down area, and he's been at odds about what to do with all the dirt.

Apparently, what he has in mind is a mini-mountain, covered with wild flowers and a waterfall cascading into a pool below. Where he's planning on putting it, we have no idea, but we'll let you know. Fair warning: Harry is a man of extremes, so with all these projects going on expect a lot of whistling followed by long bouts of cursing.

KELLY'S CORNER

It must be spring. This morning we were greeted with optimism and good cheer from our lady of fitness, which presented itself in the form of a note that simply read, "If you use the weights, I'd appreciate it if you would return them to the racks when you're done." As unbelievable as it may seem, that is the unedited version. The most startling thing, obviously, is the phrase, "I'd appreciate it," which implies that she's asking, which is not something she has much experience with. We don't know how long this will last, so don't push it.

THE HOT SEAT

We really hate to do this. We don't like putting new residents in the hot seat, but because nothing else has worked, we'll see if saying it publicly gets better results: Benji, we admire your passion for prospecting, but you simply must shelve the metal detector unless you take it off-sight. We know how much you enjoy showing it off, but enough is enough already. The incessant beeping is driving people crazy. Also, if you're planning on digging up Harry's Kentucky blue grass, you should also plan on spending your afternoons fishing your detector out of the river.

GUEST COLUMN

I want to thank everyone for their support during my war on clutter. It's been hard, but with the help of my grandkids, I have cleared out the guest bedroom. Turns out I have a pretty nice sitting chair I had completely forgotten about. Now on to the dining room! Ultimately, I have Ms. Nina to thank. She pointed out the ridiculousness of it all when she came to dinner and had to sit on a stack of LIFE magazines.

--Roger Avry

THE SUGGESTION BOX

You have spoken and we have listened. Usually when we come across a suggestion like this, we simply toss it aside and roll our eyes, but since it's such a nice morning, we've decided to think hard about why we don't think it's a good idea to put in a two lane bowling alley. Never mind the expense, which we're sure is outrageous. What we keep coming back to is the billiards table that everyone pleaded for a few years ago and that is now mainly used as an elaborate end-table. There are a few of you that still partake in the game, but your numbers have been steadily dwindling. Besides, bowling is loud and involves ugly shoes. But we're feeling democratic this morning, so we'll put it to a vote. All those in favor of putting in a bowling alley raise your hands . . . That's what we thought.

HOLY MOSES!

We're not sure where the miniature rubber tractor tire came from, but it's a big hit with Holy Moses. Unfortunately, this comes with a warning. The way Holy slings it down the hallway and then tears after it can be hazardous to your health if you're not paying attention. Also, seeing him doing this might give you the impression that he wants to play fetch. This is not the case. If you take it from him and throw it, he will be annoyed. If you try to take it from him again, he will politely remind you that he is bigger than you. If you're silly enough to do it again, well, you will join that distinguished group of things that have been pounced on and mauled enthusiastically.

FINDERS KEEPERS

Those of you that just got done reading the last bulletin will recognize the hero of our next story. Benji Little made the hot seat a record twelve times in eleven months, but instead of including all twelve entries, we've decided to tell the full story here.

Before we get started, Benji is no longer with us. Not in a bad way. He moved to a delightful, though lesser, community called Birch Pines in order to be closer to his son. If we ever found ourselves in a similar situation, we would require that the son move closer to us, but that's just how we roll.

Benji's prospecting tool of choice was the FX-458 Gold Digger X-treme Model 2 Metal Detector, which he had special ordered out of the back of a treasure hunting magazine. He was so proud of it that he had his initials engraved in the handle for an extra fifty dollars. He loved it so much, in fact, that when the ground was frozen and too hard to dig, he moved his prospecting operation inside.

Benji's passion for treasure hunting was evident from the start. During orientation, he suddenly veered off course and made a b-line for the old Victorian home that sits on the southern edge of the property. When Beverly caught up to him, he was caressing the bricks and wondering out loud about the possibility of secret passageways. When Benji learned that the home was mostly used for administration purposes and not open to the public or to residents, and was therefore off limits to treasure hunters, he took to the halls outside his room instead.

According to the incessant beeping of the detector, our little home was overflowing with treasure. The one problem being that almost all of the treasure was still attached to people. In one notable instance, Benji chased Ms. Mathers down the hallway, and when he finally cornered her, he tried to remove the silver hoop earrings from her ears and the gold bracelet from her wrist. When she screamed and struck him with her purse, he exclaimed, "Finders keepers, for crying out loud!"

One of his more egregious offenses took place the morning Mr. Thomas returned from the pool and found Benji going through his dresser drawers. When Mr. Thomas confronted him, Benji offered him one of the watches he had found. Staff and visitors had their own stories, and Midnight, if she could talk, would recount the afternoon Benji chased her with the strange pole-like object because something in her new collar had set it off. She only managed to escape because Kelly had suddenly appeared and told Benji that if he knew what was good for him he'd get that stick thing away from her, distracting him long enough for Midnight to make her getaway.

As with most things, Holy Moses had an entirely different relationship with Benji and his metal detector. Benji and Holy had formed an early bond. During orientation, Holy introduced himself, like usual, by running full speed at the new residents in hopes of making them scatter. And Benji, by happy accident, yelled, "Holy Moses! What a dog! Would you look at that!" This confused Holy to such an extent that he stopped in mid gallop and turned to Beverly for an explanation. When she laughed and shrugged her shoulders, Holy sat down and studied him.

Holy found Benji so interesting that he spent most of his free time following him around. This gave Benji the mistaken idea that Holy would like to join him on his prospecting adventures once the weather warmed up. He even went so far as to think that maybe Holy would like to carry some of the supplies. Unfortunately, Benji didn't tell anyone about his plan to turn Holy Moses into a pack mule, so no one had an opportunity to warn him.

The second week of April was warm and dry, so Benji went to an outfitters store and found a pack intended for a donkey. Holy was used to seeing Benji carrying around odd objects, so the pack didn't immediately raise his suspicion. Poor Benji hadn't yet learned that you don't force Holy Moses to do things. If you want Holy to wear a backpack, for instance, you must first offer it to him as a gift. Once he's taken possession of it not only will he wear it but you'll never get it off of him. Benji hadn't been around long enough to know any of this, so he did what most people would do and sneaked up behind Holy and threw it over his back.

Holy interpreted this as an attack and turned with surprising agility and took Benji out at the knees. Before Benji could get to his feet and protest, Holy had made off with the metal detector and was parading around with it. His rabies tag set the detector off, startling Holy, who now thought of the Gold Digger as an elaborate squeaky toy that needed its squeaker removed.

Here we most sympathize with Benji. Most of us at one time or another have found Holy Moses chewing on something we'd rather he not be chewing on, and have come to the sobering realization that we are in no position to do anything about it. We find ourselves saying, "Drop it!" in a way that comes out more like, "Drop it?"

The detector had to be sent to a shop in Golden to be fixed. In the mean time, we suggested that Benji take his box thingy down to the river and pan for gold or rocks or whatever.

"First of all," Benji said, "it's a sluice box, not a box thingy. Second of all, the river is too high. If I try to pan it I'll be swept away for sure. " So we suggested he take his box thingy down to the river and pan for gold or rocks or whatever. A bit mean-spirited perhaps, but he really left us no choice.

The detector came back three days later. To prospect in peace, Benji spent most of his time scanning the river banks. He didn't have much luck. All he managed to find were a couple of bottle caps and a bullet casing. Because of this, Benji slowly started creeping towards where the open space ended and the Kentucky Blue Grass began. In his defense, he did ask us if the maintenance department would mind if he dug around in inconspicuous places, to which we laughed and said, "We don't have a maintenance department. What we do have is a maintenance man that would start twitching uncontrollably at the mere mention."

The first hole on the property showed up in one of the garden beds. We found Harry scratching his head, looking at a shallow hole next to the tulips. He was attributing it to a rabbit, but he couldn't figure out why the hole didn't go anywhere. Harry had yet to notice that the land just beyond the property line looked like it had recently been overtaken by invisible prairie dogs.

The second bit of evidence that Benji was digging where he shouldn't be came the morning when Harry tested the sprinkler system and found water bubbling up through the grass. When he dug down, he found that one of the lines was split. Harry thought it had cracked from age and wear, but we knew better.

Over the next several days, Benji got sloppy. Where he'd previously taken great care to cover his tracks, he started partially filling his holes and throwing the little square of removed turf back haphazardly. But his big mistake was when he accidentally left his little prospecting shovel next to one of the dig sites.

Harry appeared in our offices unable to speak. He held the little shovel out in front of him. Every time he tried to say something, his voice caught. To save Benji from ending up in one of his holes, we told Harry we would take care of it. We cornered Benji and told him that if he insisted on spending his mornings digging in places he shouldn't, he should plan on spending his afternoons fishing his detector out of the river. He promised he would go back to the open space, but the next afternoon we caught him digging out in back of Harry's maintenance shed and we about had a collective coronary. Luckily Harry was tending to some indoor repairs and wasn't there to see it, but he noticed the evidence later in the afternoon and vowed daily patrols of the grounds and promised to install security cameras and motion sensors until the perpetrator was caught. Such was Benji's obsession that none of this dissuaded him.

And so the cat and mouse game began. Benji knew Harry was patrolling the grounds and carefully recorded the times and routes in a little spiral notebook. He tried some detecting between patrols, but with so much activity, he was worried that a resident or visitor would turn him in. To avoid this, he started detecting at night, but it wasn't long before Harry added extra evening visual patrols using night vision goggles. When Benji learned of this, he began breaking the prospecting into two parts to minimize his time in the danger zone. The first night he'd use the detector, but instead of digging when he got a hit, he'd mark the promising spots with little flags, then he'd come back the next night with a flashlight and do the necessary digging and sifting.

Some of you might be wondering why we kept Benji's identity a secret. We would like to say we were trying to protect Benji, but the horrible truth of it is that we were enjoying ourselves immensely. It was like tuning into a real life soap opera every day. The thrill of the hunt, the suspense, the strategy, the threat of violence was good stuff. And it wasn't like Benji was doing any real damage. Holes could be filled in and turf could be replaced. Besides, if we had turned him in, you wouldn't be reading this delightful story.

After a few days, Harry was beside himself. Every morning when he got in, there'd be evidence of digging and he would spend the morning carefully replacing the turf and grooming it until it blended in. It took him two or three days to catch onto the flag system. He still couldn't seem to catch Benji in the act, thought, so he changed his strategy.

Harry knew that his movements were being tracked, so one evening he left like usual, but instead of continuing home he parked his truck in the little turnout across the river and made his way back on foot under the cover of darkness. When he reached the fitness center, Harry saw the little glow of a flashlight and heard the unmistakable beeping of the detector, and he called out, "Hey there!" but he'd made his move too soon. Benji switched off the flashlight and disappeared around the side of the building. By the time Harry figured out which way he ran, Benji had made it around the building, through the lobby, and to his room.

Benji might have gotten away with it if Holy Moses hadn't been in the lobby looking for Ritz crackers. Holy holds grudges, and they aren't limited to living things. When Holy breaks something he prefers it stay broken, so when he saw Benji run by with the metal detector, he was annoyed and gave chase. A moment later, Harry burst through the lobby door and started down the Buena Vista wing, where he found Holy barking and scratching at one of the doors.

Harry patted Holy on the head, thanked him, returned to his truck, drove home and went to sleep with a little smile on his face.

The next afternoon when Benji was in the restaurant, Harry used his master key and slipped into Benji's room and stole the FX-458 Gold Digger X-treme Model 2 Metal Detector. The noise that erupted from Benji upon returning to his room and discovering it missing was akin to that of a mother who has just witnessed her only child being swept over Niagara Falls.

We don't actually know what Harry did with the detector. Of course Benji knew who took it, but he never filed a formal complaint. He continued taking his little box thingy down to the river, but he'd return later in the afternoon looking glum. A couple of times he came back soaking wet, suggesting that he went diving just in case Harry had indeed thrown the detector in the river.

As for Harry, he had an added spring in his step the days and weeks that followed. He filled in all the holes he could find and replaced the turf with a smile playing at the corner of his mouth. Every now and then he'd laugh.

Sometimes we swear we hear the unmistakable beeping of the FX-458 Gold Digger X-treme Model 2 Metal Detector late at night, but we can't be sure. Harry's been doing a lot of digging in back of the maintenance shed. He says it's a new project, but we're not so sure.

THE LAST STOP BULLETIN

THE WEATHER FRONT

El Nino's older brother, Tee Nino, will be stopping by this week to give us a dose of fall, winter, spring, and summer, a combination seldom seen even in Colorado. Thirty-six inches of snow will fall, then driving rain, then hail, causing mass casualties of all that is green and pretty. This will be followed by record high temperatures. Flooding is likely, also riots and probably looting.

YOU OUGHT TO KNOW

A mountain lion has been spotted several times peeking in windows late at night. Don't worry, though, he seems tame. We're thinking about naming him Bubbles.

ACCORDING TO ROGER

Have I told you lately how amazing, inspirational, and beautiful the Chin-wags are? I complain about them a lot, but if I'm reincarnated, I want to come back as a Chin-wag.

Notes from the Maintenance Shed

Harry has designated this a trash free-for-all week, so go ahead and toss your garbage on the floor. Harry will get it later.

Kelly's Corner

Kelly's note this morning had little hearts and smiley faces on it. It read, "You all are simply amazing. You inspire me to be less mean. I'm working on it. Just know that I love you."

The Hot Seat

Benji has struck gold! He's in the hot seat because we're jealous. Betty, too, made the hot seat because of the pink coat with the ruffles on it she wore the other day. It might be the most offensive thing we've ever seen. In the future, please try to pick your clothes better.

The Suggestion Box

You have spoken and we have listened. There are always a handful of you this time of year that suggest we put in an outdoor swimming pool and our answer is always, "Why would we put in an outdoor swimming pool when we have a perfectly good inside swimming pool?" Alas, we have come up with a solution. We are going to have the perfectly good inside pool drained and moved outside.

GUEST COLUMN

Let's give a big hand to the Chin-wags for their creativity and spunk!

HOLY MOSES!

Midnight, Holy Moses, and a squirrel named Johnny are getting along famously. If you want to see them rollicking, be out in the courtyard tomorrow at noon.

P.S. In case you haven't figured it out already, it is indeed April Fool's. We were just going to give a false weather report and leave it at that, but we started having so much fun we couldn't stop. Roger even pitched in, but his entry lacked the necessary ridiculousness for April Fool's. Of course he wants to be one of us. As for the real bulletin this week, we've decided there isn't enough going on to warrant the killing of any more innocent trees.

THE SENIOR GAMES

While Benji and his metal detector were both gone by the end of April, their influence carried over into May, where they played a prominent part in the outcome of the first annual Field Day, officially dubbed The Senior Games.

The original idea came from Byron, our former Olympian in residence. Bryon competed in the 1956 Olympic Games at Melbourne. He didn't medal, but he did have two fourth place finishes. To most, placing fourth in the world at anything would be cause for celebration, but not to Byron. In Byron's world, there are only winners and losers. And because he lost, he's spent every day since trying to make up for it.

To say Byron is competitive is the understatement of the century. The activity doesn't matter. It doesn't even matter if the person he's competing against is aware that he's in a competition. If you're out walking the paths at anything faster than a leisurely pace, for instance, Byron will do his best to lap you. If you're working out with twenty pound dumbbells, Byron will grab the forty pounders and mimic your movements. Sometimes he'll whistle while he's doing it, just to make you feel extra silly.

Byron trains every day. Working out, he says, is what people do to feel better about themselves. Training is what people do who actually want to get better. He has no patience for people who don't understand this distinction. One of our favorite Bryon quotes is: "Why would anyone watch television when they could be doing push-ups?" And he's serious. People like Byron don't need fancy equipment or personal trainers to motivate them. In Byron's world, hedges become hurdles, rivers become lap pools, and unsuspecting residents become human logs that can be scooped up and run with for distance and time.

Because of all this, it's not surprising that Byron has his detractors. But it doesn't seem to bother him. Perhaps he's like Samson and draws strength from his hair, which seems more flowing and voluminous with each passing year. This requires those of us who have adopted shorter hairstyles to try and hide the fact that we've been losing our hair for years to hate him a little bit.

Byron also has a condition that requires him to strip off his shirt and flex his pectoral muscles at the least provocation. He says he overheats easily; we say cow pucky.

Almost everyone has found themselves in some sort of unexpected competition with Byron, so when he suggested actual events with judges and ribbons, the reception was less than enthusiastic. Most suspected, rightfully so, that Byron was using this as a way of officially declaring his physical superiority.

This put us in an awkward position because we liked the idea. There was no denying that Byron would likely sweep the events and do a fair amount of gloating, but it sounded like so much fun and was so outside the norm of what was expected of us seniors, that we found ourselves lobbying for the games.

"We'll pick the events," we said. "That way Byron can't tailor them to his strengths." No good. "We'll announce the events six weeks in advance to all participants except Bryon." Still no good. It wasn't until Bryon agreed to give head starts of five seconds in running events and two feet in events for distance and height that the majority ruled in favor of The Senior Games.

The games were held on the first Saturday in May. We were informed by Roger P. that this is also the day the Kentucky Derby runs, so next year we will move the date to the second Saturday in May so our equine enthusiasts don't have to choose between the two events.

Byron was out before dawn, running drills and performing various calisthenics. The thirty-or-so other competitors started wandering in wearing florescent shirts and wild hats fifteen minutes before the first event was set to begin. Some of the braver contestants wore yellow headbands like Byron's and openly mocked and taunted him. Byron seemed agitated by this sudden lack of respect, but he did and said nothing.

A lot has been written about "the zone." It refers to an elusive state of peak performance sometimes referred to as "flow" because of its seemingly effortless nature. It is a state of consciousness that increases focus and allows for optimal performance. Byron, and other top-level athletes, have the ability to get into this state at will. Unfortunately, sometimes they come out of this state as quickly as they got into it, descending into a tailspin of monumental proportions.

The first event was the hundred yard dash. It was obvious from the start that only half the competitors were taking it seriously. Just before the start whistle blew, Mr. Marley suddenly announced that he needed to return to his room to change into appropriate footwear. The start was further delayed when Ms. Theron's cell phone rang, and, after digging it out of her bra and answering it, announced cheerfully that it was a wrong number. In total, Byron got in and out of his running stance six times before the whistle blew and the race began.

As agreed upon, Byron waited a full five seconds before launching himself after them. It was obvious that Bryon would easily catch them. His strides were long and confident, his arms pumping rhythmically at his sides. And then Byron decided that the spectators should behold his physique and began trying to remove his shirt. Exactly what happened we don't know, but somewhere along the line Byron's shirt got twisted and hung up on his chin, leaving him blind and zigzagging wildly. Perhaps this is why he didn't see the small hole leftover from Benji's prospecting days out in front of him. The hole wasn't large, but the lame attempt at replacing the turf left a lip the perfect height to catch Byron's foot and send him flying. The story going around is that he flew twenty feet, but the truth is that he was airborne for twelve feet and skidded along the grass for the other eight.

Byron was so disoriented by the whole thing, that when he righted himself to continue the race, he was pointing in the wrong direction. What got him turned around was Mr. Thomas, who was winning but slowing considerably because he couldn't stop giggling.

In a valiant effort, Byron turned and dashed after them, but he only managed to pass Ms. Theron, who had found out the hard way that having ample bosoms doesn't make for a pleasant running experience and had slowed to a walk, and Mr. Gentry, who had inexplicably veered off course and was trying to make his way back inside the cones.

When Byron threw himself over the finish line, the anguish was written all over his face. Both knees were bleeding and clumps of grass jutted out from under his headband. He had managed to get his head free from the shirt, but one arm was still hung up behind him in a sort of makeshift sling.

The next event was the long jump. Byron took off at such a furious clip that the angle of his body was fast approaching horizontal by the time he reached the predetermined launch spot. He panicked and leapt too early, traveling in an angular trajectory, missing the sandpit altogether, and landing hip first in the grass.

The winner of the long jump was Mr. Billings, who performed an awkward, mid-air skip to the tune of three feet. The other three competitors got scared on the run-up and bailed out before jumping. Byron, even with his mid-air problems, would have won by almost two feet, but because he had landed outside the sand, was disqualified.

Byron was starting to unravel. When things start going wrong, there's a tendency to expect things to go wrong, and since you tend to get what you expect, it only went downhill from there. There is no doubt in our minds that Byron would have won the shoe kick event if his shoe had managed to leave his foot. But, in his earnest to get a win under his belt, Byron had forgotten to untie his shoe. The kick was so forceful that his leg went up, up, up and over, taking the rest of his body with it.

Next up was the hula hoop competition. If there was one event we all felt he was vulnerable in it was the hula hoop, but we thought he'd at least make it interesting. He didn't. He lasted just twelve seconds. When the hoop spun down around his shins, he made little effort to get it going again. It was still good enough for third. Ms. Theron gyrated her way to an easy victory. True, the bosoms that were such a hindrance in the running events proved an unfair advantage by the way they prevented the hoop from falling below her chest, but it was such an entertaining performance that no one complained.

The last event was the three-legged race. We had high hopes for Byron until we drew names and found that little Ernie was Byron's teammate. Byron and Ernie are almost complete opposites in both build and temperament. Where Byron is tall and lean and powerful, Ernie is short and round and has small feet. Ernie is also terrified of Byron. When the whistle blew, Ernie was so uptight that he recoiled and almost toppled over. He recovered, though, and the world's oddest couple started their awkward journey. For the first twenty yards, they seemed to get into a good rhythm. It helped that three of the other four teams had already fallen down and were struggling to get up. Byron was so excited that they were out front that he began praising Ernie: "Good boy, Ernie! Steady. Find the rhythm! There it is. Atta Boy! Good job!" and Ernie smiled and laughed, and together they zigzagged down the field. The spectators, too, became excited and began cheering and clapping and yelling, "Go Ernie!" and it looked like they were going to win. But being the center of attention is not where Ernie is most comfortable, so the louder the crowd cheered the more off balance he became. Byron's instructions became stern: "Come on, Ernie!" Byron shouted. "Focus!" Ernie responds even more poorly to being yelled at and promptly fell down.

The Marleys passed them, but started their celebration too early and went down in a heap five feet from the finish line. Byron stood up, "Get up Ernie! Get up, for crying out loud! Get up!" and when Ernie got halfway up and fell back down, Byron grabbed hold of Ernie's leg and began dragging him. The rules state that both teammates have to cross the finish line, so when they got close enough, Byron grabbed Ernie by the seat of his pants and threw the both of them over the finish line for the win, earning him his one and only blue ribbon, and ending the first annual Senior Games.

With such a heroic finish, the other mishaps were all but forgotten, until now, of course. Ernie got a ribbon, too, which he still wears pinned to his shirt on special occasions.

We doubt very seriously that future games will be as entertaining as the first, but we're trying to figure out a way to get Holy Moses involved, so it's entirely possible.

The Last Stop Bulletin

The Weather Front

This is the time of year when we start getting annoyed that Colorado doesn't ever make the top ten states with the best weather according to the weather folks. It's hard to believe considering Colorado is supposed to have over 300 days of sunshine. Before we start writing letters and getting out of hand, though, we thought we'd confirm the rumor. We're sad to report that the number isn't quite accurate: Colorado only averages 255 days of sunshine. That's it, we're moving!

You Ought to Know

With all this talk about fishing, we thought we'd put in our two cents. But first, we'll clear up a few things. Yes, you need a fishing license. Yes, the Fish and Game people really do patrol the river from time to time, and, yes, they will fine you. No, we don't know how much it is because we've never been silly enough to get caught.

Now, while we enjoy fishing as much as the next person, we aren't alone in our thoughts on bait fishing. The problem, as we see it, is when the fish in question swallows the hook, which then has to be dug out with pliers. Not that getting a hook in the lip is any walk in the park, but when the hook is dug up from the depths, it tends to bring things with it that were never meant to see the light of day, subjecting the fish to unnecessary agony. Of course, we can't keep you from using salmon eggs and the like, but we just thought we'd give you something to think about.

ACCORDING TO ROGER

Today's lesson: Stop the commentary!

You know that little voice in your head that is constantly judging your behavior, telling you what you should do, and then yelling at you and beating you up when you don't do it? Well, it turns out that that little bugger can be shut up pretty easily using a couple of techniques.

Right now, stop reading and look around you and find everything red . . . Notice how everything quieted down? When you focus on something in your environment, it takes you out of your head. That little monster just needs something to focus on. Another one you can do, which is just as wacky as it sounds, is to close your eyes and try to feel the bottom of your left foot without touching it. Don't try to do this while you're walking or that little voice will start telling you how dumb you are.

NOTES FROM THE MAINTENANCE SHED

Some of you have noticed that all the gardening books are missing from the library. Fear not! Harry has taken them home to study. It turns out that our handyman wants to take his gardening to a whole new level this year. We also noticed a book on aquatic aerobics in his stack of books . . . We have no idea what that's about.

KELLY'S CORNER

Kelly tries to kill you in the gym because she loves you and wants you to live a really long time. We know this because she told us yesterday out of the clear blue sky. We don't know what prompted it, but apparently someone made her feel bad, which isn't easy to do. You probably shouldn't make a habit out of it, though: guilt is anger's little brother.

THE HOT SEAT

Obviously many of you didn't read last week's bulletin all the way to the end, because if you had, you would have learned that the "Notes from the Maintenance Shed" column, which encouraged you to litter, was part of an elaborate April Fool's joke.

So, just for the record, there will never be a trash-free-for-all day as long as Harry is still alive. You all had so much fun throwing your gum wrappers on the floor and leaving your beverage cans lying all over the place that we can only speculate that you had a rough upbringing which you are now acting out on.

We might have let it go, but some of you tried to blame us, which is laughable, and still others criticized Harry for being so sensitive about trash. Good lord, there's a reason we've made the cover of SENIOR LIVING three times.

GUEST COLUMN

War and Peace! *War and Peace*! *War and Peace*! Who's up for it? I've decided to tackle all 1,455 pages of Leo Tolstoy's masterpiece, but I think I'm going to need some support along the way. All the weird names really get to me, so I'm looking for a reading buddy or two to help me through the rough parts. Let me know! I've got several copies available, so you don't have to worry about buying one . . . Come to think of it, we could take turns reading it out loud, might be fun.

--Ms. Nina Anne Parker

THE SUGGESTION BOX

You have spoken and we have listened, but chef Amato is not interested in cooking any of the fish you might catch, even if you offer to share it with him. He prefers to get his fish from the store. That way he doesn't have to see it when it had eyeballs. Being a hardened chef you'd think he'd be desensitized to that sort of thing by now. Maybe it's a French thing.

HOLY MOSES!

With summer right around the corner, we thought this would be a good time to bring this up. During the summer months we tend to get a whole gaggle of new residents, not all of whom are comfortable with Holy Moses, so we need your help. We all know that Holy puts strangers through some sort of selection process. It's his standard operating procedure to be suspicious, so here's a few things to tell new residents that might make the transition easier. The best way to make it through the selection process is to offer him gifts. He's not a huge fan of dog toys. He will take them, but will often immediately spit them out and walk away. Some people think that a dog wanting to fetch is some universal trait. If it is, it ends with Holy Moses. If you throw something, he will make you feel silly by sighing and walking in the opposite direction. The fastest way to get on his good side, of course, is with cheese, so they might want to pick up an extra block or two when they're at the store.

Also, please reiterate that when Holy sits down and starts thrusting his paw at them, he isn't trying to be cute. He wants cheese, preferably medium cheddar.

THE HOLY MOSES FITNESS CHALLENGE

B y the end of May it became apparent that Holy Moses was carrying more than his fair share of junk in the trunk. This, as it turns out, was mostly our fault. When we had all of you suggest to new residents that they offer him cheese in order to get on his good side, it backfired on us. We don't know how much cheese he ate, but it must have been considerable, because by the second week of May his lust for the stuff had obviously diminished. He'd still eat it, of course, but not without a reluctant sigh.

We don't mind a chunky Holy Moses. He's adorable, whatever his girth, but we were starting to worry about his health, so we decided to put him on an exercise regimen.

We have Ms. Watson to thank for it, who enlightened us and inspired this suggestion box column:

You have spoken and we have listened. It is rare that we take a suggestion, fawn over it, and then implement it without editing, but this is one of those times. Holy Moses seems to be getting bigger every day. So, besides the obvious, "Quit giving him handouts every time he swats at you," which is easier said than done, Ms. Watson has suggested something that's been staring us in the face all along.

While handouts obviously contribute to Holy's weight problem, the real culprit is his inactivity, which is only going to get worse the closer we get to the dog days of August. As far as we can tell, Holy divides his time between sleeping in the lobby, snoozing outside by the purple bush, and sitting next to various tables in the restaurant. Our point is that Holy needs to be more active, and since he's unlikely to take it upon himself to become so, we're going to take turns walking him around the mile fitness loop every morning at 8 a.m. For those who want to participate, there will be a sign-up sheet in Reception. All of you howling about the early start time please keep in mind that we don't care. None of this is about you or your comfort. 8 a.m. is the time Holy usually wakes up and starts trying to decide if he should get up and go to the bathroom, or if he should sleep in a little longer, so we are going to help him with this decision by springing the leash on him. We've heard that the best time to exercise is before you have time to talk yourself out of it. We figure this probably applies to dogs, too. At the very least, it will allow him to do his exercising in the cool of the morning instead of the heat of the day.

Ms. Watson, since this was your idea, you will go first. Just know that he might hold this against you later.

DAY 1

Because Holy pretty much has the run of the place it never occurred to us that he might actually want to be walked. A little excitement was to be expected because of the newness of it, but we weren't expecting him to hop (yes, you read that correctly) around, taking out end-tables and lamps and potted plants.

Harry was in the lobby changing light bulbs at the time and witnessed the whole thing. We have never seen our disgruntled maintenance man laugh that hard. He had tears streaming down his face, even as he was cleaning up the broken glass and sweeping up the potting soil.

It took several minutes and the help of four people to get the leash hooked to Holy's collar.

We must apologize to Ms. Watson. What no one counted on was the weight discrepancy between Holy Moses and little Ms. Watson. No one thought for a minute that Holy would break into a run, but that's what he did, dragging poor eighty-seven-pound Ms. Watson behind him.

Luckily Holy got distracted by an abnormally large sun flower and came to a halt before Ms. Watson lost her balance and went down. Things were a little less entertaining after that. Holy didn't have the stamina to keep up the pace and slowed to a leisurely trot.

In an attempt to make things easier we sent Randy to the pet store to see if he could find a harness big enough to fit Mr. Moses.

DAY 2

Holy's enthusiasm diminished some, but only slightly. This might be due to the fact that it was Ernie's turn to walk him. Holy is naturally suspicious of Ernie, but when he saw the leash, he pushed all that aside and managed to sit still in four second increments. It only took fifteen of these increments to get the leash attached to his new harness, during which Holy became impatient and began barking in Ernie's face. Ernie is already nervous around Holy, so this didn't help.

Considering Ernie's relationship with Holy, we were surprised that he had signed up to walk him. In a well-crafted note, Ernie explained to us that this was part of his plan to become bolder. Nothing like jumping in the deep end, but we must applaud him for stepping out of his comfort zone. He also stated his hope that this would improve his relationship with Holy. Whether it has or not is up for debate.

The mile loop was generally uneventful. There was one tense moment when Ernie tried to get Holy to speed up, but they both made it back in one piece. It was all Holy could do to drag himself back to Beverly's desk, where he promptly slept through the afternoon.

It was obvious that our boy needed a day or two to recuperate, so we gave him the weekend off.

DAY 3

Monday morning didn't start out so good. When Mr. Johnson approached him with the leash, Holy rolled over on his back, and when he tried to attach the leash, Holy suddenly turned into an angry honey badger. In the end, it was Beverly who had to get the leash on him and coax him outside. Once he got going, Holy continued on with no problem, but at a much slower pace than usual, thus proving what Kelly has been telling all of us for years: exercising isn't difficult, it's putting your shoes on and starting that's the hard part.

Mr. Johnson had the bright idea to use cherry licorice to bribe him, but Holy soon became frustrated with the small chunks and eventually knocked Mr. Johnson down and happily ate the entire bag.

DAY 4-6

The novelty was starting to wear off, so we decided to change it up by walking the loop in the other direction. This bought us some time, but by the end of the third day, Holy had discovered his innate ability to turn himself into an immovable object. Beverly was still able to get him out the door, but once outside he would sit down and dare the walker to try to get him moving. This obviously amused him because the harder the walker tugged and nudged, the faster his tail wagged, the little stinker. After a few minutes of this, he'd give in and continue down the path. However, it wasn't long before he'd sit down and start the whole game over again.

DAY 7-10

It was now obvious that Holy wasn't going to continue his walks unless all of his favorite people joined him and egged him on. This worked the most consistently because Holy loves being the center of attention. But after a few days, the facility was starting to suffer: Kelly was missing her exercise classes, Harry was getting behind on the mowing, and visitors were left to fend for themselves because Beverly wasn't at her desk.

It was frustrating on our end, too, because there was no way to track Holy's progress other than visually. He had started associating the scale with exercising, making it nearly impossible to check his weight.

We tried cheese for a few more days, but because he had been inundated with cheese the weeks before, he quickly lost interest. We moved to sausage links, which worked, but because he required a link every ten feet to keep him moving, the added calories pretty much undid whatever exercise he was getting.

Holy's quest for physical fitness lasted just ten days. We had to learn yet again that Holy only does what Holy feels like doing. If he's ever going to get in shape, it's going to have to be his idea.

In a surprising turn of events, we started hanging his leash and harness up in the lobby where he could see it, just in case he had a change of heart. And while it doesn't happen as often as we'd like, he does walk up to it from time to time and look around expectantly until someone comes along and takes him out.

He is healthier these days. He's not going to be pulling sleds or competing in agility events any time soon, but he has taken some of the "Holy!" out of Holy Moses.

THE LAST STOP BULLETIN

THE WEATHER FRONT

This is the time of year where the weather has a tendency to even out, making it tricky to come up with weather reports that are interesting. This week we decided to dig around for some interesting weather statistics. It got tedious, though, and we lost interest. As far as we know, the weather is going to be just great this week. Unless it's not, of course, or maybe it'll just be partially great.

YOU OUGHT TO KNOW

It's been a while since we took a trip to the casinos in Cripple Creek, but ever since they put in that new fancy pants hotel the slots seem tighter than ever, so we might go to Black Hawk and Central City instead. The drive would be longer and the casinos would probably be more crowded, but if everyone is up for it, we'll have a go.

ACCORDING TO ROGER

Today's lesson: Be happy. It takes less energy.

You know what else takes less energy? Bait fishing. (Seriously, do you even read the bulletin?) I have nothing against river fishing, but I spent more time trying to untangle my line and free the lures that got hung up on logs than I did actual fishing. Also, if anyone has an extra pair of waders, please let me know. The ones I bought on sale were apparently marked down because they were no longer waterproof. (Serves you right.)

Today's second lesson: You get what you pay for!

NOTES FROM THE MAINTENANCE SHED

We've spoken to Harry about not starting the mowing until after eight o'clock. He was out there at a quarter to six this morning, so we know your pain. He gets excited this time of year. He starts tuning up the mowers and edgers and trimmers in April, so this has been building for a while.

KELLY'S CORNER

"Don't be afraid of the weights!!!!" We actually cut down the exclamation marks by half. The note went on to say, "There's a rumor going around the women circles that if they get anywhere near the dumbbell rack they're suddenly going to have bulging biceps and a bulging Adam's apple. You know what builds lean physiques in women? Weight training. You know what builds Adam's apples in women? Steroids, so stop worrying about it!"

THE HOT SEAT

This week's hot seat has taken on a whole new meaning. There is a time and a place for being affectionate with your spouse or partner or whatever you're calling them these days, but when the affection spills over onto the pool table in the activities room during a dart tournament, we must politely ask you to take that sort of thing to the privacy of your room. Yes, Aster and Ruby, we are secretly jealous of your rekindled passion and romance, why do you think you've landed in the hot seat. Duh.

GUEST COLUMN

Hello everyone. My name is Nina Hartley. I'm new here and I just wanted to let everyone know that I have quite a lot of knitting experience, so if anyone needs some pointers, I'm in room 17 of the Aspen wing. There will be a small fee, but it'll be worth it, I guarantee it or your money back! I also have an assortment of sweaters and socks for sale, so come check them out!

(We cut out the rest. We included this as a shining example of what not to do in the guest column, or anywhere else, for that matter. The only reason it doesn't also appear in "The Hot Seat" is because she seems like such a nice person. We've been told that we're too fast to rake people over the coals, so we're trying the kinder, gentler approach. For starters, Nina, nobody likes a sales pitch. No one. Not ever. Even if you have the world's greatest socks and sweaters, nobody wants you pushing them on them.

This is our advice: start wearing said sweaters and socks, and if someone asks where you got them, by all means tell them that you sell them. If they are truly great, word will spread and you'll have all the business you can handle. As far as charging people for knitting pointers, we're not inclined to be quite as gentle, so we'll cut ourselves off. Just let it be known that it strikes us as bit distasteful.)

THE SUGGESTION BOX

You have spoken and we have listened. Yes, Darla, offering classes on different types of dance is a wonderful idea. We're surprised we didn't think of it ourselves. We are looking into it. By the way, we know it was your suggestion because of your unbreakable habit of littering all your correspondence with little hearts. Just for the record, you are adorable!

HOLY MOSES!

Holy Moses is going on tour. The Porter Elementary third graders who visited last Tuesday got it in their little heads that it would be fun if Holy Moses visited them at their school. It seems they had so much fun crawling all over him and tugging on his good ear that they want the other classes to have the same opportunity. This is just further evidence that our boy is a mix of contradictions. We can't in good conscience recommend crawling all over him and tugging on his good ear unless you're under the age of twelve, though, so don't get any ideas.

SUMMER

THE LAST STOP BULLETIN

THE WEATHER FRONT

Leave it to Colorado to try and jam every possible type of weather into one week. For those of you that thought it was summer, you'll be right until Wednesday when the temperature inexplicably drops thirty degrees. We just hope the trees and plants don't get confused and drop dead. Thursday will bring snow flurries . . . We'll write that again: Thursday will bring snow flurries. Yes, you read that right, and, yes, it's still June.

YOU OUGHT TO KNOW

We knew this day would eventually come, and here it is: the library is maxed out. There are so many piles and stacks and shelves of books that even after we removed the furniture, it was still hard to move around. So, as much as we hate getting rid of books, even the bad ones, we're going to have to trim down the herd. We're going to place a couple of bins outside the door for the books that we're keeping, so go in and pick your favorite one or two and we'll donate the rest to charity.

ACCORDING TO ROGER

I'm sorry to say that archery isn't as easy as it looks. I had it in my head that it was just a glorified form of darts, but this is clearly not the case. It's a whole lot more dangerous than I expected. I apologize to the group of walkers that had to dive out of the way of one of my wayward arrows. I was just trying to find some fun outdoor activities to do this summer. So it's back to the drawing board. Anyone up for croquet?

Today's lesson: Try something new . . . just be careful where you aim it.

NOTES FROM THE MAINTENANCE SHED

Those who thought you saw Harry relaxing on the porch swing with a glass of iced tea and the book, *Zen and the Art of Motorcycle Maintenance*, actually did. We asked him if he was sick, but instead of answering us, he said, "What is the nature of Quality? I mean, really?" This confused us and scared us so we left him alone. We've never read this book, but apparently it makes a deep impression on disgruntled maintenance men. We saw him later in the afternoon walking around aimlessly, reading passages out loud and throwing his hands around. The grass is starting to get long, so hopefully he's about finished.

KELLY'S CORNER

Not to alarm anyone, but Kelly has recently purchased a hundred yards of PVC pipe, which strikes us as weird and mildly threatening. She's having Harry cut them into six-foot pieces. Kelly doesn't have hobbies outside the gym, so we can only speculate that all of this is for you. We tried to bring it up, but all she said was that Monday's workout was going to be a humdinger.

When Kelly starts using words like "humdinger" and laughing a lot, you know it's going to be bad.

THE HOT SEAT

How to say this politely . . . We said up front that we were going to leave the guest columns unedited and unabridged because we thought that due to the relative age of the contributors most of you would understand how to use a comma. We see now that we were mistaken. It started off okay, but as it's gone along, you've gotten sloppy, so please get your grand kids to proofread your work before submitting it.

GUEST COLUMN

We (the Marleys) would appreciate it if whoever keeps stealing our balcony seats in the theater for Friday night movies would stop it. We funded its construction, after all. Something you all are in no position to do.

(We have spoken to the Marleys and reminded them that just because they paid for the balcony seating doesn't mean that they have exclusive rights to it. That being said, if the Marleys are up there, you might want to find other seating. They like their space, so if you sit next to them, their sighing is liable to interrupt the movie.)

THE SUGGESTION BOX

You have spoken and we have listened, we just didn't like any of your suggestions.

HOLY MOSES!

Whatever has happened to Harry, Holy Moses seems to be the main beneficiary. Between readings, Harry is now pedaling Holy Moses around in the little trailer hitched to his mountain bike. He does this a few times a year during the warmer months, but it's usually just for entertainment purposes. This morning is different. They've been doing loops around the facility for almost an hour now. Every time they go by, Holy pleads with us to make Harry stop, proving that you can indeed have too much of a good thing.

WIDE LEFT

The summer started off with a bang. The Guinness Book of World Records people stopped by our little abode to record an attempt by our very own George Bevel, who looked to set the juggling world on fire by beating the previously held record of juggling four balls for two hours and forty-six minutes.

To really appreciate the significance of this, we must go back to the New Years Eve party the year before where George— admittedly inebriated—vowed to break the record the coming year as one of his New Year's resolutions. Of course, he also vowed to start reading French poetry in the same conversation, so there was no way of knowing if he was serious. It didn't help that he had reached that point of intoxication that makes speech tricky, so those who heard this declaration weren't even sure they heard him correctly.

What none of us realized was that, over the previous year, George had been secretly getting good at all sorts of things; he just wasn't making a show of it. He was also starting to harbor some pretty lofty opinions about juggling and other forms of recreation. "There's a certain beauty in virtually any activity," he told us. This seemed a bit hokey, but we let it slide. But when he went on to say that juggling was an art form that needed to be studied in order to be appreciated, we scoffed, because that's what we do best. "Art," we said, "should be held to a higher standard. What's next, vacuuming? Surely there is an art to vacuuming!" And here we launched into an original vacuum dance until he suggested we get our heads examined and walked away. We have not gotten our heads examined, just so you know. The beauty of it is that you never know which of us is the crazy one.

According to George, only about five percent of the world's population is anywhere near proficient at juggling. Quite the handy statistic to have around when your juggling is met with a shaking of the head and an awkward smile. Such is the countenance of someone trying to figure out why you're going to all the trouble. This is the camp we fall into. "If you're going to juggle," we told him, "at least juggle chainsaws or something on fire to make it interesting." Our point being, of course, that people will hang around longer if they think there's a chance you'll accidentally lob off your arm or set your hair on fire. We stand by this argument, but it has flaws. Risking losing a limb or spending whatever time you have left in a burn ward to entertain a bunch of people who are only watching because of the tragedy they might be witness to is even sillier than juggling balls, which we've already established is pretty darned silly.

But this story isn't really about juggling. It's about learning new things. Up until recently, George had believed whole-heartedly that talent was the overriding factor in any endeavor. George believed, for instance, that unless you leapt from the womb juggling, you'd never be a good juggler. Of course, we now know this is nonsense. This idea of god-given talent has held more people back than you can whack with a wooden spoon. Like with anything, there are exceptions, but they are often the result of physical attributes that are glaringly absent. If your height, for instance, peaked out at four-feet nine-inches, good luck playing in the NBA. But this isn't necessarily the point. Just because you're never going to turn professional certainly doesn't mean you can't become great at basketball.

George's epiphany about all of this came at the tipping point of a later-in-life crises. George had settled down into a life of the same thing at the same time every day, and he was frustrated, but he didn't know why.

That evening, his wife (whom George would like to remain nameless, though most of you know her) was sitting across from him, angrily knitting the fourteenth sweater of the Christmas season, when George inadvertently hurled his glass of hot cocoa at her, not only ruining the sweater she was working on, but the one she was wearing as well. Thankfully the cocoa had cooled somewhat, so a trip to the emergency room wasn't added to the night's festivities.

What had caused George to react so enthusiastically was a little piece in the newspaper about a woman who had taken up chess in her seventies and was now ranked 74th in the world. And that's when it hit him: you could learn to do pretty much anything you wanted, provided you put in the time and effort, and it didn't seem to matter when you got started.

Like most people, George figured that whatever skills he then possessed were the only ones he was ever going to have, but that evening, in dramatic fashion, he realized that he had been wrong and he laughed out loud. This coincided with his throwing his cocoa on his wife, who considered this small act of unintentional violence the final straw in a marriage way overdue for final straws.

But don't worry about old what's-her-name. This ended up being the best thing for the both of them. Though she moved out and into another community, George has learned through mutual friends that she has taken up ballroom dancing and is sorting out an addiction to bad television. The fact that old what's-her-name was trying new things was further evidence that the biggest problem with their marriage had been that they were both tremendously bored.

The whole thing was astonishing to George. How many people, he wondered, were doing things only because that's what they'd always done? He was shocked when he looked back over his own life and realized that it had been little more than a bundle of habits, and not all of them good. His life up to that point had required very little thought; his day to day activities being performed more or less on autopilot. It had never occurred to him to change, because it had never occurred to him that he could.

When he truly embraced this idea, he was faced with endless choices and opportunities. It was ridiculous. He had always wanted to play the piano, for instance, but somewhere in his brain it was hardwired that in order to be good at the piano, you had to start when you were three. He had wanted to study medieval culture in college but had gotten talked into a more sensible degree and hadn't given it a second thought since. Now, this seemed a great tragedy. Who says you can't study medieval culture just for the heck of it? He couldn't think of a time when he had learned something just for the fun of learning it.

Time, too, suddenly held new significance. "For the love of god," George told us. "There are twenty four hours in a day, and I spent most of my life doing activities that killed time. Killed time! Can you imagine? Now I can't get enough of it. I only sleep five hours a night, yet I find myself disappointed when I get tired. I've got three bookshelves full of books on topics ranging from world history to the nature of the universe that I haven't even gotten to yet."

Given George's chosen reading material, the first activity he tackled might seem trivial, but he did it for personal reasons.

Darts is usually considered a barroom game without much merit, but at The Last Stop, as most of you know, it is taken very seriously. George had a somewhat prickly relationship with the game so he never participated in the annual tournament. Every time he threw one of the silly things, it veered left and bounced harmlessly off the wall. The fact that it was always to the left was a never-ending source of amusement for his fellow residents, who crowded on the right side of the board every time it was George's turn. George was a hit in the activities room, just for all the wrong reasons. And it seemed like the harder he tried the worse he got. On one memorable occasion, George was so determined to at least hit the board that he released the dart too early and threw it behind him. The crowd roared, and so it went.

It got to be like a sideshow. The more he missed, the more people cheered and laughed, and the more they laughed, the worse George performed. Being of a jovial nature, George didn't mind a little harmless fun at his expense, but there was a part of him that wanted just once to show all of them who was who at darts.

The first thing George realized was that one of the reasons he was terrible at darts was because he was expected to be terrible at darts. So he decided to experiment. The lady from the newspaper story had learned to play chess at seventy, so why couldn't he learn to play darts at seventy-seven?

One night, after everyone had gone to bed, George went down to the activities room determined to get better. He focused as hard as he could, trying to will the dart into the bull's-eye, but the more he concentrated, the worse he did. Part of George's problem was that instead of concentrating on hitting the board, he was concentrating on not missing. It's like playing golf: if you tell yourself, "Whatever you do, don't hit it in the water!" your attention is on the water, so that's where the ball goes. It was the same with George, only his chatter was, "Whatever you do, don't throw it left!" and the dart invariably soared wide left.

After he realized this, he went back the next night, and a funny thing happened. It was not a raving success, but he did manage to clip the board once or twice. The real surprise came when he was getting ready to leave. As he was shutting off the lights, he noticed one of his wayward darts lying on the floor. He picked it up, and, without giving it much thought, threw it in the general direction of the dart board. It took a minute to register, but the dart not only hit the board, but was sticking out of the bull's-eye. George took the dart back to his room and tried to figure out what had happened.

George determined the problem was in his head. He was thinking too much. He knew from his interest in sports as a kid that in order to perform well you had to be relaxed. All this focusing and concentrating was tensing him up. His other problem, he figured, was a lack of consistency: sometimes he threw the dart with a jerking motion, sometimes he threw it sidearm, sometimes he followed through with the throw, and sometimes he jerked his hand back as if he had touched something hot. The first thing to do, he decided, was to determine the correct way to throw a dart.

At the library, he found a book with the clever title *How to Play Darts*. It was full of charts and diagrams and talked endlessly about trajectory and acceleration and proper throwing technique. He learned, for instance, that to hold the dart properly, you first had to find the dart's center of gravity. He learned all kinds of things that had never even occurred to him. He learned that you should always try to arch the dart into the target instead of trying to throw it forcefully in a straight line. He learned that you should never make a fist with your throwing hand, and that you should fan the fingers that weren't involved to keep them out of the way. He learned that you should always stand with one foot forward and balance the majority of your weight on the ball of your lead foot, and that the shoulder and torso should remain in a fixed position.

During the same trip to the library, he came across a biography of the basketball coach, John Wooden, and learned about the importance of drilling the fundamentals until they become second nature. He also read books about snipers and various martial arts disciplines and learned how to control his breathing.

Armed with this new knowledge, he returned to the activities room every night and forced himself to throw one hundred darts with each hand. Each throw was made the exact same way. The set up, the stance, the angle, the force of the throw, was always exactly the same.

After thirty days of complete immersion, not surprisingly, George could beat the local competition with either hand.

All this he kept under wraps until the second annual darts tournament the second week of June. People were already snickering about the fact that George had entered at all. The activities room was packed with eager spectators, a good deal of whom were there to see how spectacularly awful George would perform.

When it was George's turn, he stepped up, smiled, took aim, and then whipped the first dart into the bull's-eye. It might as well have been heat-seeking. No one even saw the trip. Everyone was so stunned that their jeers abruptly died along with their smiles. George looked around. He was waiting for the applause, but it didn't come. He attributed this to shock, so he gave them a moment to compose themselves before tossing a dart into his left hand, spinning around in a circle, and then sticking the second dart next to the first.

He turned to the spectators again, and not only were they not cheering, they were obviously put off by his showboating. His virtuoso was lost on them because they were anticipating a big laugh and he wasn't giving it to them. They're disappointment was overshadowing whatever appreciation they might have had for his skill. George smiled to himself. He knew what to do.

His next throw not only missed the board, but somehow managed to stick in one of the ceiling tiles. The crowd clapped. His next throw toppled end over end before landing in the punch bowl. The crowd roared. With his final throw, he managed to pin Ms. Thatcher's hat to the wall. The crowd howled and whistled and patted him on the back. "Maybe next year, George!" they told him.

We had to tell you that story in order to explain what happened when George went for the world record juggling attempt. George applied the exact same learning principles and discipline to juggling, so we were optimistic about his chances, but it was apparent from the start that he was in trouble. He threw the first ball too far out in front of him so he had to chase after it, which threw his rhythm off completely. But instead of being upset or flustered, George started to giggle. His brother, Simon, who had flown in from Florida to witness the attempt, thought this was hysterical and began heckling him and stomping his feet, which only made George laugh harder. "Don't you dare drop those little blue balls, Georgie!" Simon yelled. "For god's sake, don't do that!"

The Guinness people were not amused. Needless to say, George did not juggle four balls for two hours and forty-six minutes. He juggled four balls for exactly three minutes and forty-eight seconds, which we think is still pretty respectable. The Guinness people were annoyed that he hadn't taken the attempt more seriously and threatened to charge him for travel expenses, but they never went through with it.

When we asked George if he was disappointed, he said, "No, not really. I had too much fun to be really disappointed. I haven't laughed that hard in a long time, and I got to see my brother, so it was still a great day. At least I've got a good story to tell. Besides, there are other records. Maybe they have one for darts."

THE LAST STOP BULLETIN

THE WEATHER FRONT

We're not sure why the poets like rain so much. They're always spouting off about its restorative qualities, and its power to chisel away at rock and blah, blah, blah. That's all well and good, but when you're on the third day of a constant downpour and the lawn chairs are floating across the lawn, we must say, "Guff Off!"

YOU OUGHT TO KNOW

Someone's been cheating. While math was not our best subject, it's easy enough to figure out that if we have 150 residents all picking their favorite two books, we should have no more than 300 books to keep for the library, yet there are several hundred books stacked around the bin, not counting what's in the bin. We knew this was going to be hard. We'd put you all in the hot seat, but we picked more than our fair share, too, so we're as guilty as anyone.

ACCORDING TO ROGER

Feeling a little blue today. Not up for a column. Stay tuned for next week.

NOTES FROM THE MAINTENANCE SHED

This is for those of you wondering why Harry has suddenly started wearing an eye patch but are afraid to ask him. He'd like you to believe that his eye was injured during some form of manly labor, but the truth is that he was out rollicking with Holy Moses and turned around just in time to get poked in the eye by a tree branch. Don't feel sorry for him, though. He told us that he kind of likes it and is thinking about wearing it permanently.

KELLY'S CORNER

We have good news! After all of your hollering about the stationary bikes and treadmills, you'll be happy to know that they are being replaced with mountain bikes. You have us to thank. We argued for the fresh air and the unpredictable terrain as reason enough for the change. We also pointed out that people were more likely to take part in riding actual bikes than walking on ridiculous revolving sidewalks or bikes that don't go anywhere. She agreed, but it didn't go over well. As a rule you should never use the word "ridiculous" when talking about any sort of fitness equipment.

Keep in mind that the bikes and treadmills aren't gone, just in storage, so if you annoy her, she'll gladly bring them back.

THE HOT SEAT

Well, Roger, you finally gave us a reason to put you in the hot seat. In case you haven't noticed, we've never missed a column, or a deadline, for that matter, because we were "feeling a little blue." If you ever feel yourself feeling a little blue in the future, go ahead and buck up little camper and get on with it. Ms. Theron has been hounding us about starting a "Sexy after Sixty" column, so you can be replaced.

GUEST COLUMN

Is there anyone out there that likes treasure hunting? If so, come by room 4 in the Aspen Wing Friday evening at 7 p.m. I've found something interesting . . . Might be dangerous, might be illegal, but what the heck, you only live once.

(Benji, we know this is you. Just because you don't live here anymore, doesn't mean you can treasure hunt when you come to visit.)

THE SUGGESTION BOX

You have spoken and we have listened. We agree that there needs to be more than one book club. Not everyone likes the "Lover's Lane" series that's been the topic of conversation for the last three months. There's no reason we can't have clubs for different genres. All interested, see Beverly for details.

HOLY MOSES!

Well, this is a new one. It seems our boy of many talents has take up a new exciting and dangerous hobby: chasing bees. Ms. Thatcher caught him going after a particularly large bumble bee the other day and managed to get herself stung trying to break them up. Maybe it's all a game and the bee is in on it. Who knows the relationship between dogs and bees? Even if this is the case, it still isn't likely to end well. While Holy would probably think it was funny to trap the bee in his slobbery jowls, the bee probably not so much. Not sure why we're bringing this up because there isn't a whole lot to be done about it. Because Harry has spent so many years beautifying this place with flowers, there is no getting rid of the bees. So, if you see Holy snapping at the air for no particular reason, try to distract him or something. If you hear howling, you'll know why. Let's just hope he isn't allergic.

LITTLE RED CORVETTE

Excitement was high for the trip to Black Hawk and Central City for a day of gambling. We usually go to Cripple Creek because it's closer, but we decided to change it up. There was a drawing for a new red Corvette at the Riviera Hotel and Casino in Black Hawk, so we thought we'd give it a shot. The cutoff for the entries was 10 a.m. You had to earn 200 points on your club card to earn an entry, so we needed to be there early to make the deadline.

Even with the prospect of winning a brand new sports car dangling out in front of them, there were stragglers. Randy, whose car at the time was a 1991 Toyota Camry, became impatient and laid on the horn, and when that didn't work, he ran inside the lobby and got on the intercom: "Attention old people! The bus leaves in ten minutes, with or without you!"

We have the stragglers to thank for the harrowing ride up the canyon. We can't excuse Randy's weaving in and out of traffic, his excessive use of the horn, or his throwing us around in the corners, but we understand the urgency and are thankful that he got us there in one piece. We're certain he would have slowed down had he heard us screaming, but he had the radio turned up so loud that our screams blended in with the heavy metal music playing.

Because of all the hairpin turns, about halfway up the canyon, Ms. Crocker turned a light shade of green and started asking around for a paper bag. She was a trooper, though, insisting we push on to the casinos without stopping. She managed to make it out of the bus and halfway to the entrance before getting sick in one of the trashcans.

By the time we entered the casino, we only had fifteen minutes to earn the 200 points needed for an entry in the car drawing. We've never seen such haphazard gambling in all our lives. Everyone was hitting the "Spin" button so furiously that it sounded like far-off machine-gun fire. By ten o'clock, everyone but Fred had earned an entry. Fred had spent so much time trying to figure out the pays on the slot machine that he only managed to earn 7 points before the deadline.

We're not heavy gamblers ourselves, but we're fascinated by the different styles of play. Some played it nonchalant: "I'm just here to have fun, so you might as well give me some money." Others tried to bully the machine into paying out. Different versions of, "Come on you mother such and such," were shouted in various states of anger. Others tried to sweet-talk the machine, which we found disturbing. If you said, "Come on baby, give me what you got," to anything but a hunk of metal, you'd get slapped.

The most shocking display was from Ms. Laverty. We've heard that gambling brings out the worst in people, but the curse words she strung together were both creative and shocking. When she started pounding both her little fists on the screen, we stepped in and pulled her off the machine before security was called.

The only two that seemed to be having any fun were the Marleys, who were playing one nickel at a time just to take advantage of the free drinks. This annoyed some. The fact that they were winning using such a conservative technique only made things worse. And the more they drank, the more vocal they became: "Won seven nickels, darling," Mr. Marley would say. And a moment later, "Just won two more!" And, just before lunch, Mr. Marley hit the jackpot. He won exactly $47. If he'd been betting the maximum he would have won $1500. $47 on a nickel is a pretty good return on investment, but it wasn't going to get his picture on the wall.

The most puzzling display came from Mr. Bentley, who performed such an elaborate combination of knocks, pats, and caresses that it took things out of the realm of superstition and into the land of voodoo. It didn't seem to be working. We could tell because the knocks got louder and the pats turned into shoves.

The Hustler Hathaway was upstairs playing Texas Hold em and was cleaning up, like always. She looked like the professionals on TV with her sunglasses and ball cap. The poor fools at the table never knew what hit them.

The lunch buffet was good, but Mr. Cooper ate all the shrimp. It was an all you can eat buffet, but the staff seemed annoyed when he piled up two of the big dinner plates with shrimp, and then went back for two more. These places count on you filling up on the cheap stuff, so when he poked his head in the kitchen to tell them that they were running low on shrimp for the second time, he was escorted out of the restaurant.

The real excitement began when Ms. Eva Parks, one of our newest residents, hit the jackpot on a Double Ladybug machine. Apparently if you get two ladybugs, a daisy, a stick, and a worm all on the same row it pays a bundle. The machine whistled and hooted and clanged its way to $755. A small crowd gathered to see what all the commotion was about, but this had more to do with the fact that Eva was yelling and dancing little circles around the machine. This didn't go over well. There are few gamblers who enjoy seeing someone else win. If you don't believe us, ask Mr. Thomas, who was asked to leave after he kicked the chair out from underneath an elderly gentlemen who had the misfortune of sitting next to him and being dealt four aces on his first hand of video poker.

There is a phenomenon we've noticed with gambling: when you win, it seems easy. If you sit there long enough, eventually you get two ladybugs, a daisy, a stick, and a worm, and the money starts piling up. This is a fallacy, of course, but it didn't stop Eva. As soon as the attendant forked over the money, she was back on her ladybug machine, hoping lightening would strike twice. We know the probabilities of this sort of thing, so we winced a little when she put in the first hundred dollar bill and began betting $1.50 a pull. Twenty minutes later, it was gone. She put in another hundred dollar bill, laughing a little and saying, "It's just warming up." This hundred dollar bill only managed to last fifteen minutes. After the third hundred, we stepped in and reminded her that if she stopped now she could still go home with a bundle, but she had a glazed over look and pointed out that if she hit the jackpot with $1.50 in the machine, it would pay $5000.

We'll spare you and jump to the end of this little catastrophe. By the time the machine had sucked up her last hundred dollar bill, another crowd had formed, similar to those that hover around the edges of car accidents and medical emergencies.

In the midst of her tailspin, Eva had been chatty and upbeat, but now that she was down to her last ten dollars, an eerie calm settled over her. Her lips were pursed and her knuckles were white. On her last spin, the crowd hushed and turned away, not wanting to watch the final display, but one ladybug fell, and then another, and then a stick, and then a stone of some sort, and then a moon, and apparently that signals the bonus round because the machine let out a whistle like a locomotive.

In the bonus round, the ladybugs turn against you. Here the game is to pick squares that either reveals credits or ladybugs. If you get three ladybugs, you're dead meat and the game is over. This gives the gambler the rare opportunity to feel as if he or she is playing a part in his or her good or bad fortune.

Eva cracked her knuckles, sighed, and then chose the top left corner. 25 credits. Since she had luck with that corner, she tried the top right corner and got a ladybug. Figuring there was no way the machine would put all the ladybugs in the corners, she chose the bottom right corner and got another ladybug. "Oh, damn it!" she said, but caught herself and smiled. Next, she chose the center square and was awarded 15 credits. She shook her head. She then chose the one directly next to it and was awarded 75 credits. Apparently Eva doesn't like anticipation, because she started punching random squares in rapid succession: 20 credits. 45 credits. 90 credits. Ladybug.

It is one thing to gamble your money and lose, but it's quite another to feel cheated. She had hit two ladybugs, a stick, a stone of some sort, and a moon, for crying out loud. Wasn't that worth something? Eva stood up. We tried to console her, but she wouldn't be consoled. "$2.70! I got the freaking bonus round! It's right there! Two ladybugs, a stick, a stone of some sort, and a moon! It's right there! It's right there!—" and then, inexplicably, we heard over the intercom, ". . . Ms. Eva Parks, please report to the winner's circle."

What no one had heard because of all the commotion was that they were drawing for the new red Corvette. "Ms. Parks, you have forty-five seconds to get to the winner's circle." The problem with going to a new casino is that you have no idea where anything is. They don't have windows. There are no points of reference. The cry went up, "Where's the winner's circle!" When it was pointed out that it was on the first floor on the other side of the casino, Eva started shuffling that way, but it was clear she wasn't going to make it.

"Thirty seconds. We're still looking for Eva Parks!"

Mr. Gregory recognized the urgency of the situation and said, "Quick, throw her in!" and rolled out of his wheelchair. Mr. Thomas, who had sneaked back in after being kicked out, wheeled the chair up behind Eva, scooped her up, and started for the winner's circle. The only problem was that Mr. Thomas wasn't much faster than Eva.

"Attention old people! Get out of the way!" Randy pushed Mr. Thomas to the side, took hold of the handles and began sprinting with Eva holding on for dear life. There was no time for the elevator, so they jumped, bumped, and skidded their way down the escalator. The chair almost tipped going around the final corner. Just as they were about to draw another name, Randy pitched Eva over the ropes and into the winner's circle.

"EVA PARKS! YOU'VE JUST WON A BRAND NEW CAR!"

And she had. We've never seen someone's luck make such drastic swings in all our lives. It was exhausting. After Eva got her wrist taped up, which she had used to break her fall, she insisted on driving the car back to The Last Stop. Randy pleaded with her to let him drive, pointing out that it was the least she could do for all his help, but she refused.

The backup of cars going down the canyon stretched seven miles. It had been years since she'd driven a manual transmission, so when she finally managed to get the car moving without stalling, she was afraid to take it out of first gear. Randy was behind her in the bus, suggesting over the loud speaker that they trade places, but she just waggled her finger at him in the side mirror.

Mr. Thomas and Mr. Cooper continued their losing streak when they thought it would be fun to pile into the Corvettes virtually nonexistent backseat and came down with cramps and a mild case of heatstroke because no one could figure out how to get the windows down. When they finally figured it out, Ms. Theron, riding shotgun, took the opportunity to hang out the window and flash the oncoming traffic. One of the cars happened to be the channel 9 news van, so Ms. Parks, Mr. Cooper, Mr. Thomas, and Ms. Theron all made the evening news.

We're planning on going back this summer.

THE LAST STOP BULLETIN

THE WEATHER FRONT

Maybe if Barbara Streisand had been here yesterday singing, "Don't Rain on My Parade," our July 4th celebration wouldn't have been ruined. The rain is leaving today, though, which figures. Maybe we'll have a July 4th celebration next weekend. One of the benefits of being retired is you can move stuff around and no one questions it.

YOU OUGHT TO KNOW

You ought to know that the lackluster fireworks display yesterday wasn't for lack of effort. Those of you that took one look at the torrential downpour in the morning and decided to stay in and play Scrabble missed out on a display of human courage and determination seldom seen outside of war.

We like fireworks as much as anyone, but we don't like loud noises and are suspicious of those that pay for the pleasure. It seems to us that you could go around hammering on a trashcan lid with a hammer and save yourself the expense, but who are we to judge?

What was impressive was the determination of a few of you to get something, anything, to go off. Spinners barely got one revolution in before being drowned out by the rain. Firecrackers quickly fizzled out. Even those obnoxious things that you throw against the ground refused to pop. A handful of die-hards spent all evening lighting bottle rockets only to have them peter out and fall harmlessly to the ground in front of them.

ACCORDING TO ROGER

My country 'tis of thee, sweet land of liberty! This week has me feeling patriotic and wanting to take up musket shooting. Anyone up for some Civil War reenactments? (We're all for patriotism, but we're not sure muskets were used in the Civil War. We'll let it go, though, because we, too, are feeling patriotic this week.)

NOTES FROM THE MAINTENANCE SHED

You might want to avoid Harry. He's depressed because the rain robbed him of the opportunity to show off his one-man-fire-fighting-brigade-backpack fire extinguisher. It also made his tough talk on fire safety seem unnecessary and paranoid. We're thinking about starting a trashcan fire later this afternoon to cheer him up.

KELLY'S CORNER

Kelly is going to hate us for pointing this out, but we're feeling brave this morning, so here goes: while she is obviously trying to hide the fact, it's apparent that she has gotten some sort of makeover. Not that she needed it, of course. But her hair is different, and unless the lighting is weird, she's wearing a touch of makeup. And her nails, while not painted or anything crazy like that, are absent of hangnails and torn cuticles. Something is afoot. Don't say anything, though. Kelly isn't a fan of complements. She always detects a sarcastic undertone, even when there isn't one.

THE HOT SEAT

Well, this is an easy one. Mr. Baker, Mr. Parker, and Mr. Cooper, we don't really know what to say. Sparklers aren't for use indoors, it says so right there on the package. We understand how disappointing the rain was, but that doesn't justify moving the fireworks display indoors. Just be glad we stopped you before you set the sprinkler system off.

GUEST COLUMN

Oh my lord! What a fireworks display! I haven't seen one that good since I was a kid. Can't wait for next year!

—Mr. Edward Lansing.

(After determining that this wasn't sarcasm, we have come up with only two possible explanations for Mr. Lansing's comments: Either he has spent the majority of his life incarcerated, or his thermos was filled with something stronger than coffee.)

THE SUGGESTION BOX

You have spoken and we have listened. In light of Mother Nature completely ruining our 4th of July, many of you have suggested we build some sort of covered picnic area like the kind you find in parks. Considering we already have a picnic area and would just have to build a roof over the top of it, this is actually a great suggestion.

HOLY MOSES!

No one was more disappointed by the absence of a fireworks display than Holy Moses, who stood by the die-hards until the bitter end, even though he was getting soaking wet. That settles it: we're going to have a makeup 4th of July celebration, it just might not be until August.

A Day in the Life of Holy Moses

8:02 a.m.

Rises. Waits for Beverly to come and smoosh his cheeks. Thinks about following her to her desk, but collapses back down and stares at us like it's our fault.

8:23 a.m.

Gets up. Looks to us to let him out so he can go to the bathroom. Ernie is coming in from his morning walk and holds the door open for him, but Holy ignores him and turns to Beverly. "Fine," Ernie says and closes the door and starts to walk away. Holy gets up and shuffles to the door. Ernie shakes his head and starts back, but Beverly stops him and lets Holy out herself. Walks the extreme edge of the grass and pees. Turns back and looks at us, apparently wondering why we're still standing there. Circles. Circles. Goes over to the lilac bush. Sniffs it. Sneezes. Hops back. Circles. Assumes the pooping position. Sees us watching and stops. Stands up. We act like we can't see him. Circles. Circles. Poops. Waits for Harry, who has appeared around the side of the building doing his morning trash/poop patrol. Harry congratulates him on how big the poop is. Holy wags his tail and tries to initiate play. Harry tells him, "Maybe later." Follows Ms. Langley back inside and sits by Beverly, who feeds him string cheese.

9:30 a.m.

The string cheese isn't sitting well. Sees the Marleys heading for the lobby doors. Falls in behind them and slips out before the door closes. Chomps a big clump of grass and begins heaving, but suddenly stops when he sees a new orientation group approaching him. One woman is already eyeballing Holy nervously. He senses this and breaks into a gallop. As he approaches, she screams. Holy's one good ear goes back and he sits down in front of her and offers her his paw. Is visibly annoyed when she tries to take it instead of giving him snacks.

9:45-10:15 a.m.

Lies down by lilac bush and people watches.

10:20 a.m.

Swings by the activities room, but finding nothing interesting going on, exits and heads for the restaurant. Ernie is the first to see him and hunkers down and conceals his plate with his arm. Ernie is a pushover. Holy knows this and heads that way. Ernie decides against holding out and forks over a piece of his toast. It doesn't have enough butter on it, so Holy only eats half and leaves the rest on the floor. "Really?" Ernie says, much louder than we're accustomed to hearing him speak. Amato spots Holy and says, "Holy, you monster, you are just in time! Clean up the scrambled eggs. Nathan has screwed them up again!"

10:45 a.m.

Back to Beverly's desk. Nap one.

11:35 a.m.

Wakes with a start. His head has been resting on Beverly's left foot, which has fallen asleep. In an attempt to remove his head from her foot, Beverly has accidentally stepped on his only good ear. This is an atrocity, but since it was Beverly that committed it, he lets it go and decides to accompany her outside while she tries to shake the life back into her foot. While he's out, he decides to poop. Harry, who seems to have a sixth sense about these things, rounds the corner and laughs and shakes his head. "Slow down," he tells Holy, "the order of poop bags doesn't come in until Thursday!" Holy is apparently amused by this because he charges and snatches the garden rake Harry is carrying and takes off with it. Harry gives chase, making hollow threats.

12:30 p.m.

Returns to the restaurant for lunch and finds the doors closed. He scratches at the door, but no one opens it. He looks around, finds us watching him and wonders why we aren't opening the door for him. Ms. Thatcher, Ms. Crocker, and Ms. Theron appear around the corner. They each in turn pat him on the head. "Did someone lock you out, Mr. Moses?" Ms. Crocker says. Holy barks. They open the door and let him in. Ernie is the only one eating meatloaf, Holy's favorite, so that's where he goes. Ernie says, "No, no, no. Bad dog," but it comes out weak. Holy paws at him. "Go away, Holy," Ernie says, but it comes out as more of a plea than a command. We decide to remind Ernie that his life would be a lot easier if he and Holy were friends, and that the best way to make friends with Holy is to give him prizes. Ernie reluctantly tears off a piece of white bread, cuts a piece of meatloaf, places it on top, dunks the whole thing in gravy and then offers it to Holy. Holy sniffs it but doesn't take it. Ernie tries again, but Holy doesn't like bread with his meatloaf and walks away, leaving Ernie with gravy all over his hand. "He does that on purpose!" Ernie says, and we have to agree. Nathan must be having a bad day in the kitchen because we hear Amato say, "Holy Moses! Where is that monster? Come in here. Nathan is cooking nothing but dog food today!"

1:15-3:00 p.m.

Nap two.

3:05 p.m.

Ms. Thatcher's great grandkids, all nine of them, take turns sitting on Holy. He yawns and rolls them off one by one. One of the little boys tugs on his only good ear, but before this becomes a problem, the boy notices that Midnight has woken from her slumber on the windowsill and he and the others bolt towards her. They trap her on the windowsill, all poking her at once and yelling. Holy bounds towards them and takes off down the hallway. They give chase. Midnight is obviously confused, as are we. This appears to be an attempt to save Midnight. Curious.

4:40 p.m.

The heat of the day has Holy seeking out his favorite sprinkler. Harry turns it on for fifteen minutes every day at five when the temperature goes above ninety. Holy has arrived early and decides to groom himself.

5:30 p.m.

Sneaks into the lobby. We try to get him out because he's still wet from the sprinkler, but he jukes and jives and escapes down the hallway. We gather troops with beach towels and give chase. This is Holy's favorite game, the stinker.

6:00 p.m.

Exhausted from all the running, Holy searches for a suitable place to lay his weary head. Ernie has left his door cracked open. Holy enters. Before Ernie can complain, Holy has crawled up on his bed and has laid his head on Ernie's pillow. Oddly, Ernie is not annoyed. We call to Holy Moses, but Ernie shushes us and gets Holy a blanket from the linen closet. Holy is snoring when he gets back. Ernie covers him up.

8:30 p.m.

We haven't seen Holy in over two hours, so we go looking and find him trapped in Ernie's room. We find Ernie in the library and ask him why Holy is locked in his room. "We're having a sleepover," he says. We immediately return to Ernie's room and rescue him. Holy has apparently needed to go to the bathroom for quite some time because he gallops to the side doors and then barks when we haven't gotten there soon enough. We let him out, but before he goes to the bathroom, he suddenly freezes. We sense something, too, and notice three sets of beady little eyes watching us. It is a family of raccoons and they have found a bag of popcorn someone left sitting on the swing. Holy barks and approaches them, but they aren't concerned. They've been around before, and they know he's slow. Holy tries stealth mode: hunkering down close to the ground. They allow him to get within five feet before they start growling at him. This is his cue. Holy will only be pushed so far. He bounds after them. They scatter, but come to a stop a safe distance away. Holy barks again. They mock him by standing up on their hind legs. Holy barks again and begins to whine. He wants to run after them, but his need to pee is more immediate. We decide to stop this before it goes any further by throwing the bag of popcorn in the trash. This seems to appease him and he lifts his leg to pee. When that leg gives out, he lifts the other one. When that one gives out, he heads inside. No way of knowing if he got it all out.

9:15 p.m.

Ernie is down at the end of the hallway in his pajamas, trying to coax Holy into his room. Holy senses a trap and sits down. Midnight appears behind Ernie and slips into his room without him knowing it. Holy sees this and turns to us like it's our fault. We pat him on the head. It's been a long day. Holy lies down and rolls over on his back. "Good night, Holy," we say, and he perks up because we have forgotten his bedtime snack: one whole wheat Ritz cracker, one thin slice of medium cheddar, one slice of pepperoni. He swallows it without chewing and drags himself over to his bed next to Beverly's desk and lies down. Sleep well, Mr. Moses, sleep well.

THE LAST STOP BULLETIN

THE WEATHER FRONT

We know there were quite a few of you planning on playing a few holes at the new Prairie Meadows golf course across the river, but unless you feel like getting zapped by lightning, you might want to leave the clubs in the closet this week. Also, stay away from Mr. Wilcox. He's been struck twice over the years, and apparently the more you get blasted by lightening, the more likely you are to get blasted by lightening. Mr. Wilcox has moved his bed away from the window and is spending most of his afternoons in the theater where the lightening is less likely to find him.

YOU OUGHT TO KNOW

Violet is back, but with a new twist. Instead of seeking out Holy Moses, she has struck up an unlikely friendship with Midnight. We should mention that Midnight's demeanor is improving by leaps and bounds. Midnight has had a shaky relationship with dogs, so her first reaction to Violet was to suddenly transform herself into a Halloween cat and hop sideways. Violet's reaction was to jump back, flop down, and roll over. This sudden show of submission apparently is the key with Midnight, who proceeded to do a drive-by head bump. This was good enough for Violet. Apparently that's all that's needed in the animal world. Midnight has been following her around all morning.

ACCORDING TO ROGER

It's all about the vibrations, people! I vibrate, you vibrate, everything vibrates! (Careful, Roger.) "The universe is your candy store. Ask and you shall receive. Seek and you shall find. Like attracts like. Worry creates more of what you're worrying about. You turn into what you think about most of the time. Focus is everything. Be grateful for what you have." That's what they say. I don't know about all that, but I do know that the one thing you can change in an instant is your attitude, and I know of no better way to do it then by dancing. So, everybody up! It's time to get your groove on! (You know that music you're hearing, Roger? It's only in your head.)

NOTES FROM THE MAINTENANCE SHED

Harry's grouchy. He's had a couple of bad days. His regular mower (big red) broke down, so he's had to mow the whole grounds with the little blue push mower with the wobbly wheel. The grass catcher has a hole in it, too, so he then has to go back and rake everything. He got so frustrated yesterday that he started cutting all the grass with a weed whacker.

KELLY'S CORNER

Well, it was good while it lasted. The kinder gentler Kelly has left the building. Those of you who were wakened this morning by what sounded like a tornado will be glad to know that it was just Kelly's wrath, and that the building, for now, is still standing. The vending machines, all three of them, sadly are not. Kelly can only be pushed so far before, well, before three perfectly innocent vending machines, guilty of nothing except housing sugary, diabetes-inducing snacks, are upended and stomped upon. We promised Kelly some weeks ago that we would start replacing the Snickers bars and Skittles with healthier choices, but we forgot.

We are busy rectifying the situation. We've sent Randy on a mission to find sugar-free gummy bears and baked potato chips. There will be a few items of the old guard remaining, but now that Kelly knows you have options, you might want to employ a lookout when hitting the vending machines.

*** This just in! Breaking news! The reason for Kelly's violent outburst has been solved and it has nothing to do with us! Whew! Apparently she was under the impression that her long-time man-friend, Chris, otherwise known as the green giant because of his large stature and love of green clothing, was going to propose to her on her birthday because he'd typed "Ringes" (poor fellow) in the Google search engine. This also explains her giddiness lately and her recent makeover. Alas, it was all for not. Instead of buying her an engagement ring, he got her a replica Super Bowl ring because he thought it would be funny. He also thought it would be funny if he gave it to her down on one knee. This, it turns out, is not funny, just ask the vending machines.

THE HOT SEAT

Well, this is a first. Our boy, the one and only Mr. Holy Moses has landed squarely in the hot seat for his behavior towards Violet and Midnight. Holy became so frustrated by their new friendship that he confronted them both in the hallway. Attacked is too strong a word, but he did show his teeth. We don't like this side of our boy. Violet wasn't impressed and proceeded to bath Midnight. Who can blame her? It's hard to take Holy serious with only the one good ear.

We couldn't bear the thought of Holy Moses being alone in the hot seat, so we've added Mr. Parker, who would have made it in next week, so it's not like we're picking on him.

Mr. Parker, we must applaud you for taking up the guitar this late in life. This personifies The Last Stop's philosophy of "It's never too late to learn," and we hope that one day you will be good enough to accompany the choir. The problem isn't with your playing, Mr. Parker, it's your incessant strumming of the A minor chord that's got everyone in an uproar. If it was a pretty chord, say G or C, it might not be so bad. (Note: in the spirit of honesty, we got help from the choir director. We had no idea that what chord he was playing, and we'll bet that most of you didn't, either, so you all have learned something today.) A minor, when you play it slow, has a melancholy about it that has everyone looking for the piano that's likely to drop on their heads, and when you strum it real fast, it feels like we're in a western movie. We don't want to be in a western movie, so please move onto something else. You've got the A minor chord down, take our word for it.

GUEST COLUMN

"At night, the shades of light dies, horribly, and without fancy care . . . Until the sun, for thou, shines in and comfortably warms thee, until I wake suddenly and without care for . . ."

I would love to hear what you all think! This is a poem I wrote in middle school, reworked of course.

You can slip fan mail under my door!!!!!

--Author, Midford Bradley

(Okay, this is your dear Chin-wags here, hence the parenthesis. We don't want to be dream killers or anything of the sort, but for the love of Jesus, this column is not to be used for stuff like this. We understand the struggling writer's need to be published at all costs, but this . . . this . . . There is so much wrong with this . . . Midford, we love you, we really do, but in case it's escaped your attention, it's 2014 not 1402 so all these thou's and thee's and what for's, good lord! And don't get us started on, "Without care for . . ." Without care for? Without care for! What in the Holy Moses is that? See, you went and got us started.)

THE SUGGESTION BOX

You have spoken and we have listened, but we won't be getting any rabbits, guinea pigs, rats, or hamsters to add to our collection of four-legged friends. Apparently gobs of you have been watching the new *Little Critters, Cute and Cuddly* series on Animal Planet, but what they left out of the title was the odor that usually goes along with them. Also, guinea pigs whistle, and hamsters look cute and cuddly when they're running on their wheels, but what you don't know is that they're trying to work off a lifetime of hostility brought on by captivity.

And while we're on the subject, we're not going to get any birds, reptiles, pigs, or goats, either. Yes, we have a horse barn, so we can't rule out eventually getting a horse, but for now, we have all we can handle in the way of four-legged creatures with Holy Moses, Midnight and the occasional visit from Violet.

HOLY MOSES!

Just a quick reminder here: Mr. Moses doesn't like being used as transportation. One of your great grandchildren (we know who it is, but since he's only six we see no reason to point him out) found out this the hard way when he got it in his little head that it would be fun if Holy towed him around on his skateboard. Our boy is pretty sharp, so it didn't take him long to figure out what was going on. When he realized he was being taken advantage of, he was understandably upset. Whether or not he should have stopped abruptly and body-checked the poor lad off his skateboard and into the hedges is up for debate, but we really can't blame him. It was hot that day, and Holy isn't a fan of heat, nor is he a fan of unnecessary exercise.

THE END

THANKS FOR READING!

Haven't read the first book? See what happens
when new management takes over and tries to change
everything that makes The Last Stop great. It isn't pretty!
The book that started it all, THE LAST STOP, available
on Amazon.com.

Join The Last Stop Bulletin for the latest news, contests, new releases, and interactive fun here:

http://eepurl.com/buXIOz

If you enjoyed Grandma vs. the Tornado, please consider leaving a short review.

THE FUN HAS JUST BEGUN!

I would love to hear from you!

kirtboyd@netscape.net
www.facebook.com/kirtjboyd
www.twitter.com/kirtjboyd
www.goodreads.com/kirtjboyd